DANCING ON A WAVE

ISBN-13: 978-1544734774
ISBN-10: 1544734778
Translated from the French original: *Danses sur les vagues: rêveries d'une jeune boutiquière sur une petite île*
Translation by Marie Lyne (née Marie-Joseph Ng Cheong Tin)
Design by Terence Leung
Illustrations by Joyce Ng Cheong Tin-Leung
Photo on page 150 courtesy of Peter Fong

For my grandchildren:
Emma, Ethan, Sienna and Charlotte.
May they, as well as all the other youngest members of the family who make up the next generation, one day benefit from its contents.

For my children Terence, Olivier and Mei,
lest they forget our roots.

For my sister and my four brothers,
that they remember the good life we lived as young children.

For my parents, Papa and Maman,
who gave us so much.

For my grandmothers, brave Hakka women, and all our Hakka elders,
whose memory we will continue to honour.

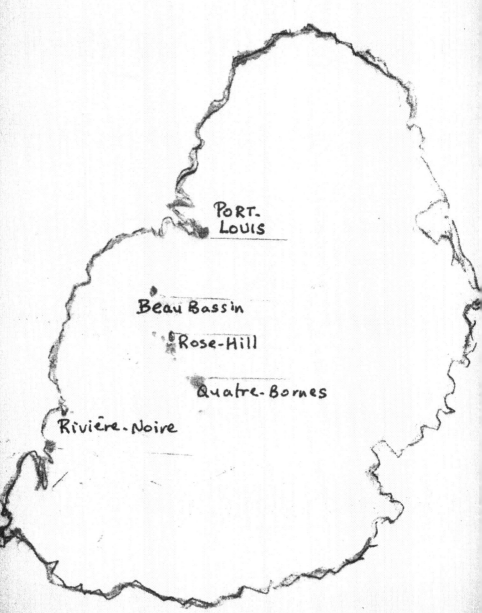

MAURITIUS

PORT.
LOUIS

Beau Bassin

Rose-Hill

Quatre-Bornes

Rivière-Noire

A dot in the Indian Ocean

Arctic Ocean

Atlantic Ocean

Pacific Ocean

Pacific Ocean

Indian Ocean

● MAURITIUS

TABLE OF CONTENTS

SUMMARY

In her new short story collection, Joyce Ng Cheong Tin-Leung preserves memories of her own childhood and offers new narratives about cultural identity and the loss of innocence. Her young protagonist is guided and protected by the vibrant immigrant community on the island of Mauritius. Leung never forgot the lessons she learned from her family and neighbors. Now, she shares them with you.

The young girl at the heart of the story has grown up in a colonial world. The island's Caucasian population lives in large mansions while the Hakka-Chinese, Indian, and Creole laborers and merchants make their homes in other quarters. Leung recalls a beautiful community that had much to give. The young girl meets the liberated women of Meixian in her grandmother's circle, hears tales of fierce female fighters in their homeland (Fengliang), and witnesses a sacred Buddhist funerary rite. At the same time, natural disaster bleeds onto the island and shocks its inhabitants. Leung's short stories provide an invaluable look at an island on the verge of social change. With a scholar's eye, she looks back at her childhood and examines the threads of colonialism, multiculturalism, community spirit, and optimism that ran through her early life.

ABOUT THE AUTHOR

Joyce Ng Cheong Tin-Leung used her own childhood on the island of Mauritius as inspiration for her semiautobiographical collection of short stories, *Dancing on a Wave*. As a young girl, she helped her family run a shop on the island.

Leung received her doctorate in French and French literature from the University of Toronto. She turned her doctoral dissertation on slavery and indentured servitude into her first book, *L'Esthétique de la canneraie dans le roman des Antilles et des Mascareignes*. Her short stories have also been included in various publications.

Leung has spent forty years in Toronto and has taught primary, secondary, and postsecondary education. She has since retired and now devotes her time to enjoying life with her grandchildren, volunteering in the community, practicing yoga, and writing. As she loves drawing and painting, she has illustrated this new collection of stories with her own delightful sketches.

FOREWORD

The little child in the texts has grown. But in these stories, it is the young girl who speaks, of a time that dates to when she was three, and older.

It is the young girl of that time who speaks, with the feelings that the reminiscence of that life brings to her. She dares not say that her narrative is the whole Truth, but what she says, she sincerely believes is the truth – it is based on the truth.

Some thoughts or comments are those of a grown up, and are interspersed throughout her writing. Sometimes a certain historical fact is inserted. But these texts do not pretend to be History, just little stories.

Please note: The spelling of Creole or Hakka expressions used in the stories is not a formalized one. And the expressions in those languages are translated or briefly explained the first times they are mentioned in the book. The in-text references are listed alphabetically, in full bibliographic details, in "Further Readings" at end of book

(March 2017)

ACKNOWLEDGEMENTS

I would like to thank my parents for the life they have given me. My deepest gratitude goes to my children (Terence, Olivier and Mei) and their partners (Janey and Jeremy) for being the mainstay and the force in my life; to my sister S. and my four brothers (B, L, J and E), and their spouses (G., P., A.Y., L., Y.), for their loving assistance and constant reassurance.

I thank my uncles and aunts, my cousins, nephews and nieces for their contribution to the text, and their support over the years. I would like to express my special thanks to Annie who has been there from the very beginning; and to those who constitute my extended family and whose presence has always been so supportive (ML and A., CM, SP, FU, LL, CL, CS, CH, LT, CC, SS, PF and VA). As well, I thank my in-laws, especially M., G., B., J. and M., for providing comfort and assistance. As well, my sincere appreciation goes to all my friends, colleagues, and compatriots for their ongoing encouragement.

My deepest gratitude to Siew, Bob, Pascale, L., Jean-Noel and Entse, Terence, Olivier and Janey, Mei, MenLeen, as well as Chantal, Philip, Lisette, and Tin, for their editorial work and proofreading. Some performed a colossal task, and went beyond the call of duty. Emma and Ethan have helped by pointing out a couple of typos, and Sienna and Charlotte by critiquing my sketches!

My heartfelt thanks to Siew for having undertaken the enormous translation project, and to Terence who has worked so hard on the book's layout and graphics.

ON BOUNDARY ROAD

I try in vain to remember the details of my childhood buried in the debris of Boundary Road, or Barclay Road, or Léoville L'Homme Road.... The disjointed snatches of conversation that I recall are without details, or importance – at least from the adult's point of view. Silhouettes and figures have become undefined contours, eroded with the passage of time. But somehow, reality can at times be perceived in its pure essence only from a certain distance, when many a year has elapsed.

The first fragment is about our childhood at Boundary Road: the smell of wood, the glazed veranda, steps, coconut trees lining the alley in the front, the spacious and sunny play-room in the back, and on the side, a room where we kept all manner of things. I cannot even remember where we slept, except that we spent a great deal of time in the big room at the back where the boys played with wooden or cardboard trains or cars. For us girls, our big delight was the one and only doll we owned, sent to us by our relatives in South Africa.

It was a spacious house, white, made of wood, built in the colonial style with plate glass windows at the front. The sitting room, being in the central part of the house, was dark. The veranda at the front faced a beautiful garden. If, after a short walk in the front of the property, we turned left, we would come to that wing of the house, where the Belleville lived. We visited them from time to time. I recall an old lady (we called her granny) and another woman, her spinster daughter, sitting in their small lounge full of impressive dark furniture that smelled, during the first few seconds of our visit, of age and mustiness. They often showed us their collection of family photographs. Among these was one of a young man wearing horn-rimmed glasses that gave him an intellectual look. The two ladies were very proud of him! His name was Charles and we are not sure if he left for France or Australia when he grew up. Later on, after many years, we came to wonder if we ever really met him? Did this somewhat mythical person actually play with us in the garden when he visited his grandmother and aunt? Or did we dream it all? We followed the journey of this Charles through the two women who told us about him every time we visited them over the years, for we continued our visits even after we had moved from Boundary Road.

Another memory is of our strolls in the big garden where there was a little grotto that sheltered the Virgin Mary and the Infant Jesus. A place that was entirely secluded. It was separated from the street by a bamboo hedge, and by an almost endless multitude of ferns where all the shades of green intermingled. This lush vegetation muffled the noise emerging from Boundary Road. The grotto felt like a quasi-sacred place, and although we were very young at the time, we could not help noticing the peace and quiet that prevailed there. The tiny shrine was shrouded by shrubbery, and surrounded by small plants decorated with small red flowers that we enjoyed popping against our foreheads. There, we also liked to look for those bushes that bore miniature water cloves that we utilized to clean our slates.

N. and C., our dear cousins, remain part of our memories of those far-off days. They were a bit older than us. They often shared our playtime and childhood games near the little grotto, thus playing an integral part in our lives. The shady canopy of the trees and the thick layer of the climbers and clingers like *liane cacapoule* or *lingres* acted like a natural barrier protecting us from the dangers of the outside world. N. was the silent and comforting presence of the reassuring elder sister, and C. liked to tease despite his quiet personality; he also liked to protect us from various dangers, sometimes real but mostly imaginary.

I cannot remember too many details about Maman and Papa other than the fact that our mom was very beautiful: always very elegant even when she wore her simple housewife dress. She was striking with her long jet-black hair, slim figure, pale complexion, and quiet smile. She was always occupied with her children, or some house work, or sewing. It was the years prior to our move to the family business in Quatre-Bornes. Papa was employed by a "white" firm in Port-Louis. It must have been at the beginning of his career as a "Graphic Artist" (this term did not exist then!) He wore a khaki suit when he went to work. He left early in the morning to catch the bus, sporting a dark grey English felt trilby, a *sapo fete*, and sunglasses that gave him a distinguished air. When he was at home, he often listened to his giant radio (with its big valves), and sometimes he put on his 78 rpm records on his gramophone. It is from Papa, and Maman as well, that we have inherited our love of music, for we were constantly surrounded by melodies or operas. Mother had memorized a few words of *Plaisir d'Amour*, a French song, which she hummed with great feeling - though she did not know the language. She usually did this while doing some house chores.

The house was always impregnated with the aroma of a Chinese stir-fry, but at some point occasionally there was added to the repertoire of Asian aromas, the strong smell of Creole spices in preparation of a local dish (a *Rougaille poisson salé*). We had just been introduced to the Mauritian cuisine. At the time a maidservant helped Maman prepare the Creole dishes since our mom, having been raised in the traditional Chinese way, did not have a clue about Creole cooking. There was always the shadowy presence of a maidservant assisting our mother but I cannot remember who it was.

My sister S. was always with me, or rather, I followed her faithfully with our two little brothers (B., L.) on our heels. I believe B. was not yet three at the time. J. was a new-born baby. It was the late 40's - or 1950. Our youngest brother E. would be born in Quatre-Bornes.

I remember a certain shop up the hill, a few steps from the house. I am not certain who owned the shop. Our brother B. remembers that it was called "LaBoutique Longaille", for the owner was tall. It must have surely been a Chinese family, for in the 40's and 50's, and even earlier, almost all the retail shops on the island (the *boutiques*) were owned and run by the Chinese community. That corner shop was important to us. We often dreamt of it, of its sweets: lemon drops (six for one cent), delicious milk fudge, pink or white or green coconut cakes. We also relished in other local treats made of ground maize, sugar, milk or other ingredients: *gato-coster*, *puddin Maille*, or *La poude maille*. At the side of that shop was found the tavern. The maid who accompanied us to the shop usually took us to that side for a couple of minutes. We were attracted to the noise and the quarrels between drunken customers, and to the nice rum aroma! A bit of an unusual hobby for such young children! Later on in life, we would all feel quite nostalgic about that shop. Decades later even Papa, when he had become blind already, asked our youngest brother to bring him there to visit the shop and that family.

Beyond that shop where we were allowed to go occasionally, accompanied by the maidservant, we knew very little of the neighbourhood. At least, not during our very early childhood. But when we were a bit older, we learned about the *Tip Top* bus that could take people further afield, in the depths of Quatre-Bornes and St. Anne, or even in the suburbs of Beau-Bassin.

It seemed to us that our home was closed to the outside world. Nobody came except for our cousins who must have certainly stayed with us on some weekends, or part of the main holidays.

However, the important visitor was Ah Bhor (Ng Bhor), Papa's mother who came to stay several times a year. She brought with her all sorts of aromas (healing balms including Mentholatum, camphor, spiced herbs and poultices). She introduced us to new sounds and voices through her conversations, and stories that she told us at night in her captivating way before we went to sleep. To our sheltered world, she brought a taste of other worlds that were unknown to us: towns and villages she had lived in or walked through. For us Ah Bhor was somewhat like a breeze which brought us the scent of a faraway garden that we had never seen, but one that was suddenly and thankfully blown to us by this new wind. More often than not, one or two of her cousins accompanied her. They walked long distances, from village to village, from town to town, to visit their children. To us, they seemed very old (although at the time they must have been only in their 50's). Their faces were ravaged by the elements and marked by the heavy work in the fields performed when they were in China, in Fengliang, their ancestral village (a small town nowadays, in the county of Fengshun). They bore the scars of the rough past of this village, when during the *Punti* wars of the 19th century, and even in later years, the women had to defend their village against the *Punti*, their invading neighbours, with all manner of weapons including rocks, stones and sticks. Then, some of them had to join the powerless villagers to defend themselves during the Japanese invasion of China in the 1930's. They had been in their own way almost "women-warriors". After all, many of them having to work in the fields, the Hakka women had in general been with unbound feet, as opposed to their other Chinese sisters who had been for at least nine centuries the victims of such an atrocious custom.

At the beginning of their lives in Mauritius, those women wore Chinese costumes. They visited us wearing their Chinese outfits (*sam foo*): trousers and black tunics, with oriental style necklines and buttons. However, later on, they began to wear westernized dresses and shoes, mostly in black and dark blue hues.

Ah Bhor, who was not very tall, had the strong and muscular appearance of a peasant woman. Years of walking and physical work had broadened and thickened her hands and feet and coarsened her skin. Her face was tanned and creased with laughter wrinkles, making her look, now that I think of it, like an Inuit woman from Canada. She had a large mouth, healthy teeth and slanting eyes that stretched out with her big smile. She embodied perseverance and endurance: virtues that became crucial for the Hakka people during the long years of their various diasporas and migrations over the millennia. In short, despite her hard life, our grandmother retained a loquacious and exuberant personality which revealed a true "joie de vivre".

Life became a little more exciting during Ah Bhor's visits. I remember the stories she told us. She talked about her early years on the island, the sea voyage on the big ship. She was already pregnant with our Papa during their long journey. She left her natal village to go to Hong Kong through the port of Shantou. Then on to the ship towards Mauritius, to her life as a new immigrant. She recounted how in subsequent years she had to work relentlessly to feed her large family of ten children. In our teens, we discovered that the shop the family bought when they first arrived on the island went bankrupt, due in part to the prevailing economic climate – the global slump of the 30's.

Apart from these visits by Ah Bhor and some other members of the family, we lived an uneventful life on Boundary Road. But one day, a bizarre and memorable incident happened which created great excitement in our family. That morning, a messenger came to warn Maman about something. Immediately following the conversation, we heard the maidservant and Maman gasp and whisper, all flustered. They ran around locking all the doors, noisily pulled all the curtains in the veranda and bolted the front door. They quickly ushered us under the big polished table in the veranda where they joined us. They were instructing us to be silent when suddenly we heard a loud and booming voice coming from the outside and shouting: "Ah kiouk! Ah kiouk! Open the door or else I will break it down!" (Ah Kiouk was Maman's name). There was not a sound from us. Despite the cramps that threatened us, we remained under the table as if paralyzed. Our childhood instincts warned us of danger. The screams and threats continued for several minutes. Eventually there was a lull and we heard the voice retreating while at the same time uttering swear words. At last we were allowed to come out from under the table. This incident is still embedded in our childhood memory: the visit of aunt X, a mentally challenged relative.

We later heard the details: the mother of an aunty had escaped from the asylum in Beau-Bassin and had walked to our house to assault us. Much later we discovered that she was schizophrenic. Poor woman....

To us children who were between the ages of one to five, everything seemed of enormous proportion. I remember the Singer sewing machine (Black and shiny) on the small wooden table that we were not allowed to touch because of the danger of overturning it. Imagine our fright when one day our younger brother L. decided to move the table from its usual place! It must have been a matter of trying out his physical strength, a small child of barely two years of age! He was lucky as the machine missed him and fell by his left arm, barely touching him (the bobbin holder scratched him lightly). He would have received a good hiding if Maman and Papa were not in a state of shock. They were only relieved that he had not sustained a more serious injury.

We have all been infested with worms at one time or another during our childhood (possibly from playing with the soil). Our mom and the servants gave us regular doses of (Castor) oil to get rid of the infestation. This was normally done in the early morning. We will never forget the *colic* spasms we suffered from the purge, and the race to the *pit-latrines* in the outhouse all day long!

I recall that the boys always wore shorts sewn by our mother, made of khaki or cotton. My sister S. and I were usually dressed in identical clothes made by Maman or one of our aunties: flouncy checked or floral dresses that came just above the knees. In the winter we wore quilted Chinese jackets. At home we always wore cotton slippers made by our grandmothers or great aunts. Handmade, the soles were made with a piece of cardboard sandwiched between layers of material. The adults wore "k'iaks" (wooden slippers with thick platform soles) made by our relatives, mainly to take their showers or to wash up. Outdoor shoes, especially the patent ones which were too expensive to throw away, were handed down from the older children to the younger ones (a piece was cut out in the toe area if they became too small for the growing toes). Apart from a very special off-the-peg dress, given to us by our family in South Africa and made of tulle or adorned with à-jours embroidery, all our dresses (blue ones for S. and pink or red ones for me) were made of cotton, and had deep hems which were let down, little by little, as we grew a few inches taller. These dresses lasted us until there was no more hem to be let down. We also inherited clothes that our big cousin N. had outgrown. Since those earliest days, I have never got used to clothes that are not comfortable on me and that do not wrap me with the softness of the old cotton of my childhood.

It seems to me that Ah Bhor was living with Coocoo at Beau-Bassin in those days. But Sessouk, Papa's youngest brother lived with us. He attended the Royal College. He was tall and thin with hair swept back in the style of Errol Flynn (with the help of a little Brylcreem, no doubt!). He was a head taller than his oldest brother. Despite that, he was frightened of Papa who treated him like a son and disciplined him as such for 20 years separated them. He always wore knee length khaki shorts and short-sleeved shirts. I seem to recall that the small bed in which our young uncle slept was in a corner of the large dining room. He studied well into the night, for our dad kept a close eye on him. He lived the modest life of a poor student. In the family lore there is a story about his shoes. When we were narrated old family stories, when we were given examples of perseverance and endurance, we were told how Sessouk had to wrap his feet in newspaper because of hardship. We do not know the specific reasons for this action - everyone seems a bit vague about it. Was it to avoid chapping for he did not own decent shoes? Were the shoes too worn for the long distances he had to walk, not being able to afford the bus fare? In short, it was mainly a matter of poverty and pride, and we children admired him for it.

As well as talking to him, we liked to observe him going about life in his calm manner. He was our role model. We were so small alongside him. We listened with interest to what he said to us for we admired his young man's knowledge. I remember his words of comfort when I suffered stomach pain. It was the day Maman and Papa were told that I was suffering from "an attack of albumen". We were in the living room and Sessouk was in front of me. The previous day, had he not been the one to point out to my parents that I had pain in my stomach and that I seemed very ill?

Our young uncle took us to the kindergarten school on his bicycle. The small school run by Miss R. was a few steps from our house, on a street that started at Boundary Road and disappeared beyond a small hill. The area up that hill was mysterious to us; this territory was out of bounds to us little children. We could only perceive from afar, through the layer of dust stirred by pedestrians walking along the dirt lane, small houses made of rusty corrugated iron sheets, thatched huts with small children in rags at the front, and hen coops alongside.

S. and I spent the day at the kindergarten. We took our packed lunch with us: bread with butter sprinkled with sugar prepared by Maman or the maidservant, together with a thermos flask of Ovaltine. Our parents eventually found out that the maid there did not give us the Ovaltine drink for lunch but drank it herself; this resulted in an onset of "albibin" (albumen) in my already anaemic system. That was according to the adults at the time, when I developed stomach pains after a year of this poor diet of bread and water. It is a mystery that S. was not similarly affected. There is no doubt that she had the immunity gained from the special care she received as a premature baby born at seven months. The two grandmothers (Ah Bhor and Young Bhor) had fed her by pressing milk from a soaked cotton ball and letting it drip drop by drop into her tiny mouth. I never had this kind of special nourishment. Hence the difference in our constitution, which meant that I was always the frail and poorly one whereas S. was the strong and chubby one.

Thus evolved our early years in the large glazed wooden house on Boundary Road. When I think of these years now, the details are indistinct. The places and characters take on a somewhat mystical aspect, for the impressions mingle and intertwine in a tapestry that seems to derive from some dream rather than reality. These old memories come back to me as if from a fairy-tale. A world where everything seems steeped in a kind of magic, an enchantment that can only be engendered by the pure innocence of early childhood.

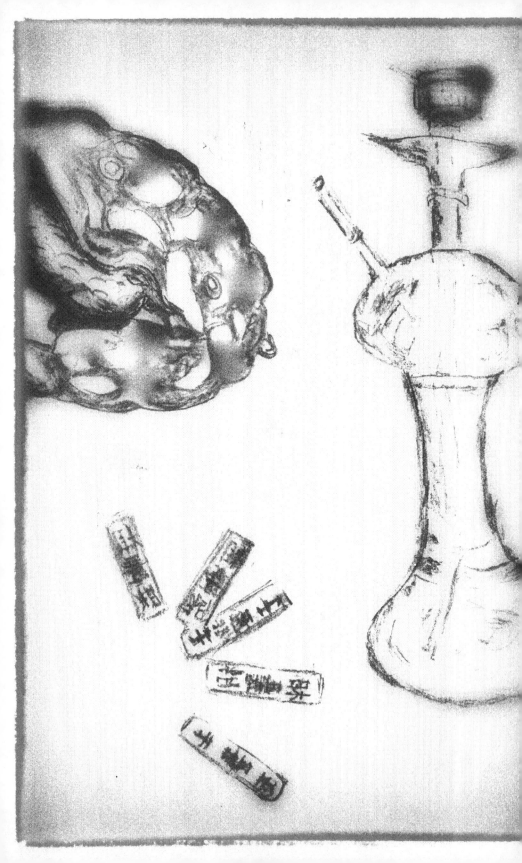

2

AFTERNOON WITH
YOUNG BHOR

When I think of my Young Bhor (Maman's mother), it is with a mixture of affection and awe. I remember her as being a refined woman; slim, petite, with a distinguished look.

In the late 1940's or very early 1950's, during our visits to Young Bhor in Quatre-Bornes, I often sat in the small veranda to look at her while she put her hair up: it was a daily ritual that was quite mesmerizing to me as a young child of about three or four.

Her black hair was always done up held with a wide hair slide, with the end flipped up. She would do it meticulously in the early morning, with some perfumed oil. Her deft hands would run her thick Chinese comb through her shoulder length hair, and swiftly flick it up into the hair slide. She would also oftentimes use her thread-and-powder method of "waxing" off the superfluous hair at the nape of her neck, so that her appearance would be perfectly neat. With a to-and-fro movement, keeping her fingers close to the neck, she would guide the thread on the powdered skin to remove any fine hair from her nape. Whatever she did for her appearance, it was a matter of extreme dexterity and finesse.

She would then finish getting dressed. She usually wore a Chinese *Sam Foo* (traditional set of Oriental jacket and pants): always black or charcoal grey. She had a figure suitable for this traditional costume. She wore the fine cotton ones for the house, and the silky ones for going out. In later years, I remember her wearing dark Western-style dresses of a simple cut and sober design. The one I admired most was made of navy blue Crêpe de Chine with very small white flower sprigs – the buttons on the dress were flower-shaped too. To me as a child looking at her, whatever she wore, she seemed to always be a figure of pure elegance and refinement.

After the early morning ritual, she used to sit and relax in her low chair in the courtyard, in the space right in front of the small veranda. She sometimes did some craft or sewing. She and her friends used to sew either Chinese slippers made of satin or cotton, or Oriental toggles that would be used for Chinese outfits.

The slippers were made of satin if they were for going out. Cotton was the material used for slippers used daily in the home. The intricate process of its fabrication was a matter of wonder to me. As children, we liked to sit for hours watching her and her small group of friends perform this craft. These Chinese *savates* (slippers) were of a great variety both in colours and in fabrics.

First, the template made of a thin cardboard was cut according to the size of the prospective owner. Then it served to cut out the sheets of cotton or satin which would constitute the shoe. The sole, in multiple layers, was cut and sewn together with the cardboard piece placed between double layers of material. The stitching was all done by hand, in a methodical and meticulous way. The final touch consisted of sewing the top band on the open-ended slippers. Sewing it in a tight fit kept the slipper snug around one's foot as if made to measure. There was an effective way of assembling all the parts, that was by combining rice glue and stitching. The thicker the layers had become, the more necessary the use of awl and thick thread. The procedure for the closed-in slippers was much the same, but was even more complicated. The result was always an amazing pair of Chinese slippers to be worn even for short strolls.

Young Bhor also made Chinese toggles. These were always in pairs since one side of the pair had to be strapped to the other side by a flap or "hook" made of the same material. She used very fine strips to form an exquisite flower-like or leaf-like base for the button.

All this work involved a good part of mid-morning to mid-day, and it was after those tasks that we children had a great time. For the afternoons with Young Bhor were very different from what we were used to in our own home. She sometimes would take us out to the market or for a stroll. Was it going to rain? Should she take her colourful Chinese bamboo umbrella? These large heavy umbrellas from China seemed to take up such a big space in her small veranda! We were happy to follow her wherever she chose to take us. Sometimes, it was the market: we loved to observe the mounds of fruit and vegetables on display, and to listen to the loud calls of the merchants. At times, it was a visit to some relative or friend of hers; most of these lived only a few minutes' walk away... What a treat for us, young children, to experience new things, and to visit new acquaintances! But the most fun for us during our stay at Young Bhor's was when she had company in the early afternoon.

For oftentimes, she had friends and family over for her small parties of *Pen Kim (or Lien Kim)*, that is a game of long slim Chinese cards based on the same principle as Mahjong. During these quiet gatherings, one or two great-aunts, like our grandmother's sisters-in-law, our Coo Bhors, smoked their little thin cigarettes or long Oriental water pipes. They seemed to be liberated women. They were certainly free spirits, now that I think of it. Young Bhor's friends and relatives did not look as if they were subservient to anybody. They appeared to do as they liked and go where they liked! Historically, there has always been the tradition of the "strong and independent Hakka woman". After all, the Hakka women, as we know, never had to bind their feet as other Chinese communities did for more than nine centuries, until the turn of the 1900's. ("Hakka Women", http://publishing.cdlib.org/)

We children were allowed to watch our grandmother and her guests play their games. The ladies were in traditional Sam Foo (Chinese costume), mostly dark and distinguished looking. They spoke in their Hakka language since none of them ever learned how to speak their adopted land's language (Creole). They rarely took any notice of us, munching on Chinese cakes and taking sips of Chinese tea in between their cigarette puffs or pipe inhalations. The small room, filled with the quiet chatter of voices, was imbued with faint smoke and vapour from the cigarettes and pipes. The conversation, held in Hakka, sounded like a soothing soft rumble to our young ears. At the time, we understood vaguely the meaning of their talks, but later we learned more about the content of these conversations. The motif rarely changed whenever these old aunties visited Young Bhor. It was a leitmotiv, mostly concerning their past in China, the reasons for their migration to Mauritius (the more recent arrivals having taken place in the 1930's or later); they seemed to have been haunted by the Chinese Civil war, which started in 1928, and by the Japanese invasion which occurred rather simultaneously for a number of years as of 1931.

Each of them spoke quietly, as if in a monologue:

We were lucky to have escaped the Japanese that week... remember how many women got raped by the Japanese troops? Was it 80,000? What monsters!

Were you frightened when you had to leave Moyenne (Meixian) and cross the forest to reach the countryside...?

What really happened: is it true a thief tried to rob T.T. of his bike while you were crossing the forest? Or was it that he got lost himself in that wood!

Then from the past, they would jump to the present-time Mauritius and their everyday routine on the island:

It is getting cold in Souillac. I have bought "kapok" (cotton filling) to make a new "Bhee Koot" (comforter)...

"Mo Siong Kon" (Not a problem)... We will help you... Not to worry... we don't mind coming to Souillac next week to help...

Ah! Did you try this squash vegetable called..." Makeh ah?? Heh a mm meh" (what is it again? Isn't it...), ah yes "Shoo Shoo ah..." (Cho-Cho); they sell them cheap at the market. Seems they make wonderful "niouk yans" (Hakka vegetable and meat steamed balls)... people say they can easily replace the "Lo Bhet" (Chinese turnip)...

"Aya... Shoo shoo ah"... I will never get used to it here... these strange veggies... and I cannot explain what I want at the "PahSak" (market)... they all speak that "Fan Fa"(foreign language) – I will never learn it – they call it "Creole", "hey a mm meh" (isn't that so)!!

... "Shoo Shoo" is much cheaper than "Lo Bhet" and not bad at all...

Such was the quiet chatter in the room. It was mainly a quiet reflection, a sort of perpetual stream of consciousness. They would move back and forth from their past in China, to their present situation of "relatively new" immigrants in Mauritius. Generally, most of the ones in the room had immigrated in the 1930's, so that there had after all been a lapse of almost 20 years since their arrival on the island. However, their generation always considered themselves more as visitors than settlers in their new country. They never accepted the sacrifice demanded by the spirit of assimilation. They all had the hope, as all the Chinese immigrants on the island did, that they would go back to China (*tson t'ong san*) to live the rest of their lives there. They kept to themselves in their microcosmic bubble - which would burst only for the next generation.

Their relaxed and moving voices formed a soothing background to their activity. At times, during these ladies' *Pen Kim* games, Young Bhor would get up and shuffle almost noiselessly to the small "coops" where she kept her silkworms. She would feed them some mulberry leaves, have a check of the webbing or silk formation in process, then come back quietly to her seat to resume her game. Whether she actually harvested any real silk thread from her silkworms, we never found out. As children, the mere sight of these worms in such small boxes was a matter of great fascination!

In the meantime, the cook prepared our supper of rice and stir-fried greens – that was the normal, daily kind of meals a Chinese family would have at the time. Simple and satisfying. We would all sit at the round table with the adults: the ladies would have gone by then, but there were the shop-helpers (the *commis*) who all ate with us.

Maman and Papa were not there with us when we spent the night with our Young Bhor. At the time we still lived in another town. We children usually came to the family business in Quatre-Bornes on occasional weekends or even a couple of days during the big holidays.

Young Bhor usually put us to bed early after supper. She would undress us; give us a quick wash (*Seh Kiok Mien*), the affair of a wash-basin filled with hot water; put our little undergarments into our panties so our tummy would not feel cold at night; then up to bed. It was an old brass four-poster, with a mosquito net above it. If there were three or more of us, she would install us in a "transverse" way (*TahVangMin*), so that all of us would fit in the same bed. The *Bhee* (comforter) was always very fresh.

She at times had a little chat with us in Hakka. One evening, she remonstrated me for having crossed the street too carelessly in the morning; I recall saying something back in Hakka, with tears in my eye since I was taking her words of caution as a grave reproach. In 1949 or 1950, Quatre-Bornes was hardly more than a village. With one narrow main road, there were scarcely any cars circulating during the quiet hours of mid-morning. There were many carts laden with canes led by a donkey or an ox, but these carts were very slow and of no great danger to children. Even at our young age, we were allowed to cross the street with a group of older kids, holding hands, as long as we looked both sides vigilantly. But that morning, I had been imprudent: it seems that I had crossed separately from the group! I was only three years old after all.

Before falling asleep, from our bed we would look out the window-panes where we saw the neighbours' mulberry tree; we vaguely observed the branches swinging lightly in the breeze; we wondered about the people who lived beyond that window. We knew that they were different from us, had a life quite strange to us, and a world remote from ours: that they were "white" and we had never spoken to them.

Sleep was slow to set in when we slept in Quatre-Bornes. With the novelty of various events and the break from our daily routine, the excitement remained with us till nighttime. We would usually turn and twist a bit before we fell into the deep sleep of the very young ones.

Such were the afternoons at our Young Bhor's in Quatre-Bornes. The town was small and a place imbued with peace and quiet, as was Young Bhor herself. She dealt with us her grandchildren with a lot of care, as surely she dealt with the rest of the world. These were moments of wonder and joy – to be immersed in such a loving, yet to us a puzzling world. When I think of these days now, it is always with a sense of great nostalgia for a past forever gone.

3

PIQUES-PAQUES

L ast night, I dreamed of Piques-Paques. I have for years wondered what the truth was, of this horrific figure, which has haunted for several decades all the children on the island. The numerous sayings about him sufficed at the time, in the fifties, to evoke fear in our minds, children and parents alike: the name "Piques-Paques" (or Pic Pac) was synonymous with terror as soon as it was mentioned. The fear of that figure - known as "child eater" - has remained acute in the collective memory of the islanders for a long time.

Many years after the tragedy (which occurred in 1951), children were still not allowed to go anywhere near La Citadelle. That ancient colonial fort located in the capital city of Port Louis was called "Fort Adelaide" by the British in 1835, and had been utilized as an army barrack then. This was where the whole "incident" had taken place. As children, we were given no details, and it was never made clear to us whether it had been the abduction and murder of a little girl, or many girls, but we instinctively knew it had been something horrendous. So, on the island, the name "Piques-Paques" had replaced the term "Lougarou" (local werewolf): it came to symbolize horror or spookiness, and was used as "scare tactics" towards children. To all intents and purposes, to us children, Piques-Paques could very well be still in the neighbourhood!

It was only when we became young adults that we found out what the "incident" at La Citadelle had entailed. It had involved the disappearance in Port-Louis, in the year 1951, of two young children, and later the finding of their bodies in La Citadelle's water tanks, only hours after the parents had declared them missing. The young children had been sexually abused and severely mutilated. According to the local authorities at the time, such violence had rarely been seen on the island. Witnesses helped in the prosecution - in 1952 - of three suspects (Piques-Paques, Le Fou and Le Roi) who were thereafter condemned to the gallows (Ces crimes les plus marquants www.lexpress.mu, 3 January 2017).

During the years following these horrific murders, the island remained steeped in great anguish. For my sister S. and me, growing up in the fifties, it was too close to home to ignore warnings from parents and authorities. We had to take extra measures since La Citadelle is behind T'ong Ha, the pagoda where our Young Bhor lived at the time. S. was at greater risk than I, since she actually lived with Young Bhor for a whole year; and to compound it all, the school which she attended (Loreto Convent) was right at the bottom of La Citadelle. The danger was not as great for me, as I would only spend an odd weekend or so in that neighbourhood during the long holidays, when I visited Young Bhor at the pagoda.

In those times, everyone on the island felt very nervous if they had to go for one reason or another in the vicinity of La Citadelle in Port-Louis. In fact, one strange and traumatic incident happened to S. and me one afternoon. It was 1956, only 5 years after the horrendous murders. In those days, in spite of everything, children of a certain age were generally deemed to be safe if they were not in the immediate area surrounding La Citadelle, and if they walked on a well-travelled road during the sunlit hours. It must have been in the summer months since it was still almost bright in the early evening. And we were walking on the other side of T'ong Ha and quite a way from La Citadelle. This fact added to our sense of security. S. and I took Rue Labourdonnais from Tante Nette's home located on the other side of town near La Montagne des Signaux, to walk from the higher grounds of the city down to T'ong Ha. We had almost reached the corner of that particular rather quiet artery to turn into the well-travelled Rue Pope Hennessy, when we felt two fat hands grab both of us and press us to a protruding belly. I can still remember the sensation of utter fright at the touch of this obese abdomen. It was a big man trying to grab and seize us; two children walking alone in this rather quiet spot. I was 10 and S. was 11. We knew by sheer instinct that we had to free ourselves fast from his grip and run for our lives.

In a flash, we realized that by kicking and punching that giant figure with all the nervous energy generated by panic, we would loosen his grip on us. Instinctively, we aimed for the intersection where the well-frequented avenue started. Pulling and kicking, we moved toward our goal inch by inch. We knew we would be safe once we were past that corner! Struggling with all the energy we could muster from our small beings, within a few seconds we were out of his grip and running like mad to the curb, able to cross the big street. The pagoda was thankfully only a few steps from that corner, and right across the street.

Had we been less energetic and panicky - for undoubtedly who did we have in mind during that split moment but the personage of Piques-Paques – the man would have easily kept his hold of us and shoved us into a waiting car nearby.

The terror we had felt in that instant was to be concealed from the adults for years. Without ever discussing about it with anyone else, not even with each other, we had unconsciously reached the consensus that silence about it was one good way of coping – and erasing it entirely from our lives. The shaking of our young bodies once we reached T'ong Ha was hardly visible to the adults that evening. It was to remain our big secret: the nightmares which we would have in the coming years, of those fat hands and the protruding belly, would be hidden from others for decades. As a matter of fact, if I remember rightly, having somehow later noticed that we were not our usual selves, Young Bhor put us to bed early that night, thinking that we had caught a chill, S. having run a temperature later on that evening.

So when I dreamed about Piques-Paques last night, it occurred to me in the nightmare that perhaps that man after all had been Piques-Paques - maybe he had somehow escaped the gallows! The dream about that terrifying figure was not clear; none of the nightmares of the past five decades has been. They have always consisted of electrifying flashes: a grabbing of our young bodies by huge hands, our run for survival in the twilight between reality and dream. There never has been a sequence of events in those dreams: these seemed to last only for one second, representing the encapsulated time in which we could have been abducted and shoved into a big van, before we reached the other side. In real life, the worst could have happened to us then. Subconsciously, our frightening experience that evening never went beyond that specific second in our existence. It simply left us with the terror of dreadful possibilities, translated and projected in our constant nightmares!

4

A School Day in My New Year's Dress

When we were young children in the early 1950's, we were granted only one new dress per year. The rest of our wardrobe consisted of "hand-downs": used clothes from our older cousins or siblings. The same applied to shoes, except that it was even worse for these: the yearly pair was not a guarantee since our siblings might not have grown out of theirs within one year. If our feet grew out of our nice patent leather shoes, we had to still wear them but with the toe part cut off, to allow more space for our protracted toes.

That particular year, I received a beautiful *tuile* (tulle) dress, white and embroidered with tiny multi-coloured dots all over. Gathered from a high waist it went down just above the knees. The top was adorned with frills from the shoulders in a V-shape, as was the fashion for young girls in the 1950's. I loved that dress. What a beautiful gift from our aunties and cousins from South Africa!

One day, that year when I turned five, I must indeed have run out of "simple" clothes to wear for school. Or else, for what other reason would I have been permitted to wear my beautiful New Year's dress for school on that particular day?

Usually, it was my big sister S. - hardly six years old - who took me to school. We were still in Rose-Hill. From Rue Boundary, we had moved to Rue Léoville L'Homme. It was before we moved to the family business in Quatre-Bornes. I remember that the walk to school was not that long: it was a question of just crossing the street, and making a right turn into Rue La Reine to reach our school (Notre-Dame des Victoires).

At the time, the school had not been renovated yet, and was still a large colonial construction, made of wood, with a glazed veranda at the front. The classrooms were large enough to accommodate at least 35 pupils with rows of desks and chairs.

Notre-Dame des Victoires was our local Primary school in Rose-Hill. All young children go to school on our island, since the Primary system is free to all. This tradition is steeped in history. After the French Revolution in 1789, there began a tradition of education for all citizens in France and other French territories. Since the island was under French rule, this tradition of "Free Education for All" began in Mauritius at the end of the 18ᵗʰ century. The British administration followed in this tradition, albeit with a slow start. A few primary schools were opened to "non-Whites" on the island, but in general education remained the domain of the Whites. However, in 1815, the Reverend Lebrun set up free day primary schools to the destitute and Coloured children in Port-Louis. It was still the era of slavery. (Kalla, A. Cader, Le Mauricien, 2 July 2014)

Catholic clergy, though slow at first, followed suit, and began to take an active interest in the education of the slaves, and later on, in that of other segments of the population. A large Indian population came as indentured labourers to replace the slaves in the 1830's after the Abolition of Slavery, and those were gradually granted primary schooling. Education in primary schools (including Christian schools) has remained free to this day.

Hence, as all the generations who lived under the British rule and even after independence, my generation benefited from a system of free education, with very large classes and a regimented approach typical of the colonial era. Teachers had to follow a rigid schedule and strict discipline. Students had to respect rules. Or else the stick would quickly make its appearance! (There was no 'carrot' in sight). It was the era in our Catholic schools of big assemblies and prayers every morning, and the morning inspection of nails, shoes, and so forth. We were the regiment, and the nuns and teachers were the army officers with their batons ready to strike our knuckles at each infraction (example: dirty nails)!

My sister S. was the eldest one of all the siblings; she had become, from the respectable age of six, my official guardian anytime we were out of our home or at school. The teachers or the principal called her whenever some problem arose with me at school. These problems or "incidents" generally concerned the checking of my dirty nails in the morning. Even worse, on one occasion, it was found that my neck was still dirty (it seems that my towel had not done a thorough job that morning!). S. was supposed to report all these transgressions to our parents after school.

One day, the nature of these reports reached a new dramatic height. A dull afternoon after lunch, I felt an urgent need to pee. I desperately wanted to ask if I could go to the toilet, but hesitated. No permission was ever granted for visits to the washrooms right after lunch since we already had been allowed to go during the break. I tried to bear it. I gradually became covered with a cold sweat and overcome with mild shivers even though my new dress was light and flimsy. Like other students during afternoon prayers, I remained standing, but I kept my legs as tight as I could. My instincts told me that this posture would prevent any "accident" from happening. I especially did not want anything to happen to my beautiful dress.

During the various lessons of the afternoon, sitting erect and holding my breath lest my bladder would explode, I looked at the board without really seeing it, my bladder having become a bloated balloon! It was at the sound of the teacher's voice calling my name that the tide swelled, and I felt that my restrained leg muscles no longer had the power to prevent the inevitable. I stood to answer the teacher's question, and lo and behold, there below, between my legs, ran a sweet and hot flow of liquid that inundated the whole space surrounding my feet!! I remember my neighbour showing this newly formed little puddle to the teacher, and the whole class gasped. I was in a state of great shock and shame. Tears blinded my eyes and I just stood there paralyzed. Dismayed, I collapsed on the bench, thus wetting and soiling my beautiful dress! The pupils closer to me stared at me with a mocking grin. The teacher was more sympathetic: she gently took me by the arm and led me to the outside door. She ran to my sister's class to let her know what had happened. It was almost the end of the afternoon session, so they allowed us to go home.

I don't remember ever apologizing to my sister for that unfortunate mishap in our childhood, and the inconvenience of it all upon her young years. I don't think I spoke all evening, to her or to our parents. All I remember were my tears. I cried profusely from the minute it had happened till night time. No words would have expressed adequately the feeling of shame, and of disappointment with myself that I felt, especially when I saw Maman take the soiled dress to rinse it under cold water.

This incident has remained with me all my life: up to the day I reached adolescence, whenever I saw a white tulle dress, I would tend to break into tears!

From that day on, my beautiful dress seemed to have somewhat aged. However, that tulle dress remained an important part of my young life. In spite of the unfortunate incident, it will be remembered as a treasured possession which had come from some foreign place, and which during several years had given such joy and pleasure to a little girl on a tiny faraway island!

5

TAVERN AND SHOP

In Mauritius, during the last decades of the 19ᵗʰ century, retail shops
became more and more the domain of the Chinese immigrants. The
Fukienese and Cantonese settlers at the early stage of that century were
followed later on by the Hakka migrants (Li Tio Fane Pineo, 1981: 88-
89). Taverns in Mauritius had gradually become an integral part of the
Chinese shops, so that before the middle of the 20ᵗʰ century, most shops
had a tavern attached to them. And since every major intersection in a
town or every village in the vicinity of a sugar plantation had a Chinese
shop, *LaBoutique Sinois*, one could find a tavern in every corner of the
island.

There had been Chinese migrating from their homeland for several
decades in the 19ᵗʰ century, and this for many reasons (economic, political, personal). However, it was in the 20th century, in the 1930's, that
a major migratory movement from China to various parts of the world
occurred, due to civil strife, and the Japanese invasion of East Asia. The
Hakka people leaving the Meixian area, and some other Chinese from
Southern China, settled in great numbers in the Caribbean, in the islands of the Indian Ocean, and India. There they built businesses in
retail, mainly on the islands, and got involved in the tannery and laun-
dry/dry-cleaning industry, mainly in India.

It was a well-known fact that the Chinese shopkeepers on our little
island – and in other parts of the world – were a hard-working community. They contributed largely to the economy of their new homeland. For example, as early as the 1880's, the Governor of Mauritius,
Pope Hennessy, lauded the Chinese immigrants' contribution to the
local economy, which constituted more than 29% of the island's revenue
thanks to the heavy taxes they paid to the colony. That revenue was in

great disproportion to their small numbers. In addition, for more than a century, practically from the inception of Chinese "LaBoutique" (grocery stores) in the regions where these shopkeepers had settled in the world, including Mauritius and Jamaica, they initiated a credit system for the benefit of their customers, allowing these to pay only at the end of the month, and sometimes even at their next pay during the cane harvest, *La coupe*. This "banking system" is still in place on the island, but to a lesser extent: the number of "LaBoutique" has decreased substantially in the past decades. The "little red book" where they listed all the items bought on credit by customers is now part of the collective conscious-ness of many communities in the Indian Ocean and in the Caribbean!

On our little island, the Chinese shopkeepers worked from dawn to dusk. Normally getting up at 4.30 a.m. they worked in the shop till 7.00 p.m. The shop owners as well as their assistants, the *commis*, con-tinued well into the night doing the preparatory work for the following day: making paper bags (cornets) from old newspapers, of different sizes, to contain quarter lb., half lb., one lb. of sugar, for example; making small packages of two - five cigarettes for those who could not afford a whole pack; cutting whole salted fish into small squares for those who could afford only one bit for supper. The chores were relentless.

All this work yielded only a slim margin of profit, not enough to provide for a number of children, let alone the whole extended family of *commis* and other employees. Thus the spirit of entrepreneurship pre-vailed in many grocery stores: the shopkeepers developed diverse proj-ects, including the making and selling of cakes, candies, roasted meats, crispies or chips, and so on. And the prospective increase in the shop revenue encouraged many shopkeepers to annex taverns to their busi-nesses. The profit would be even larger if they sold *gajacks* (appetiz-ers) with the drinks. This is why one would witness from the crack of dawn the preparation of these *gajacks*. The shopkeeper and his wife or some other employee would make all manner of appetizers, succulent and spicy enough to encourage more drinking: local buns, *pains-maison* stuffed with sardines and pickled chili, fried slices of bread garnished with chutney, fried pieces of liver or salted pork, deep-fried chicken wings, and so forth.

The tavern was usually a medium-sized room where workers from various industries and sugar plantations came to relax with their friends on weekdays after work, and on weekends. There they were served grogs of our local rum from neighbouring sugar estates and our local wine, *Di Vin LaClosse*. My brother J. recalls that many of these drinkers would dip their small finger in their drink, then shake off a drop or two to the floor, as an offering to the ancestors, they would say.

Every evening in our shop in the little town of Quatre-Bornes, as in most Chinese shops on the island, the noise in the tavern became intolerable: the chaotic din was caused by the drunkards, their disputes and their abuses. Sometime during the evening, say, between 6.30 p.m. and 7.00 p.m., things came to a head: swearing turned to blows.

At the end of the evening, when all the money had been spent on grogs, it was necessary for the drunkards to choose one of the group to settle the bill. Whenever the miscreants had to pick a "privileged payer", the fighting renewed in intensity. The person selected would categorically refuse to pay! That was when there was a stampede towards the street, the drinkers leaving the premises without paying for the last grogs.

At our tavern we saw a whole variety of drinkers. Among them, there was a Mr B. who had fought in W.W.I. He was an acquaintance of Papa's. At age 70, he was healthy-looking and rode his bike to the shop. He loved having a piece of Tête de Maure cheese with his rum. We also saw a Mr R., a sergeant with the Police Band (best band on the island), who agreed one day to play his flute for our little brother E. These gentlemen were issued their monthly "rations" (groceries) at the tavern counter for it was there that moderate-income clients ordered their monthly provisions. Among those drinkers was a personage known to us all as "Pierre Le Grand" (big bully) – nicknamed thus by the inhabitants of our town. He was quite a personality, famous not only for his chronic state of drunkenness but also for his great intelligence and charm. Always with a sardonic smile and a mocking gleam in his eyes. He was pleasant enough to us children. In fact, we had mixed feelings when we were with him. We were fascinated by his brilliant ambivalent personality, but at the same time, we were apprehensive as well, in case he would have one of his "drunkard" fits in the middle of our conversation.

Pierre Le Grand was dark in complexion, and was considered a "Creole" (that is, of mixed descent, including African). He considered himself mainly Black. He never referred to his White ancestry, though we guessed that he was partly White. He often referred to his Black community, the remote past, *zistoires lontemp*: he talked about things which happened so very long ago, that had affected and he claimed, "continued to affect and paralyze his people". We realized later in life that he was referring to the era of slavery when millions of his people were imported from Africa and vicinity, to the Caribbean and the Indian Ocean, to work in the plantations. Some historians believe that there had been more than 17 millions slaves from Africa for the trans-Atlantic slave trade (Trans-Atlantic Slave Trade, www.unesco.org), and several millions for the Indian Ocean slave trade (Slave Route: Trade in the Indian Ocean, www.unesco.org). This monumental human tragedy lasted for four centuries: from the 16th to the 19th century. That had been the sad fate of his people, he said. His people had thence lost its soul and identity. However, as he uttered, the choice to become a "drunkard" was his alone; it was nobody's fault or responsibility but his.

Dark and big, Pierre Le Grand was strong, belligerent, and adamant about not paying his bills. He mostly counted on his drinking mates to pay for him, but at times even the best of his friends abandoned him. That was the kind of scenario that was at the source of big fights in Chinese taverns. And the shopkeepers, who most of the time made a living through intense hard work, could not let the drinkers have their way.

In our shop, Salon and Tambi acted as the "enforcers of justice" at the Tavern. They - and Papa, if he was available - were the ones who ran after the drunkards. The team was very prompt in their reaction and was soon in hot pursuit of the miscreants. At odd times, one of ours may have had a scratch or two from a broken bottle tossed at him that had brushed against his ear or cheek. However, most of the time, we saw the return of our team unharmed and proud of their role as "defendants of justice". In short, Salon and Tambi (and Papa) constituted quite a formidable team.

Salon and Tambi were both quite strong physically. However, they differed in appearance and personality. Salon, of medium build and wiry, was of light brown complexion, neatly dressed but always barefooted.

Tambi, of stocky build, was of very dark lustrous skin and dressed in only a vest even in winter. The former was introverted, with a quiet smile and chuckle underneath his moustache, while the latter was outgoing, with a joke always readily available for others to enjoy.

Salon and Tambi were both Tamil. Their community numbered several thousands on the island. Later in life, we came to understand why they were so proud of their Dravidian culture; it was 4,000 years old at least! They spoke Tamil, one of the dozens of Dravidian languages spoken by millions of people in the world. Some Tamils in Mauritius descended from independent skilled craftsmen who had migrated to the island for the making of tools or the like. But Salon and Tambi probably descended from indentured labourers who, when slavery was abolished in 1835, had been imported from India in great numbers to replace the slaves on the sugar plantations. Around that period, during four decades, the British imported a total of about 400,000 Indians - a minority of whom was of Tamil religion (Li Tio Fane Pineo, 1984: 168-69). These indentured labourers, though not legally imported as "slaves" suffered a very hard life in their plight as indentured labourers, and this lasted more than a century (Li Tio Fane Pineo, 1984: 98).

Tambi and Salon participated in the ceremony and procession of Cavadee in the summer months. On the day of the feast, the devotees had to bear for several hours the pain inflicted by the multitude of needles piercing their skin in traditional patterns: tongue, forehead, cheek, torso and so forth. We as youngsters watching this impressive procession from our shop doorsteps often wondered about the suffering and forbearance of these faithful. But we learned later that they did not actually feel much pain thanks to the amount of fasting and meditation warranted before the ritual.

We were also fascinated by another Tamil ceremony called "Walking on Fire" where the faithful, after a long fast, could walk on live embers without getting burned!

As their ancestors had done during the preceding century, Salon and Tambi worked assiduously all day. It was a habit that had become part of their mentality and their being. They were the ones to unload from the merchandise truck the heavy sacks of rice and barrels of salted fish or metal containers of oil and petrol, to place them in the *La samm marsan-*

dises (warehouse). During those strenuous jobs, we could see the sweat on their foreheads. For decades they were required to pull a hand-driven cart to deliver merchandise to customers, that is their "rations" which they purchased from us every month: big litres of oil or petrol; bags of rice, dhal, lentils, flour, sugar, salt; big bars of soap used for the laundry. There were also cans of Corned Beef or sardines for those who could afford such things.

Later, when we came to own a bicycle, they had some respite. The bicycle gradually replaced the cart near the shop entrance. They began riding the bike to the clients' homes, loading it with big *tentes* (hand-woven carrier-bags), filled with the customers' "rations". After many years, they no longer had to sweat so hard, for we bought a van. This van would transport bigger and heavier items to the well-to-do customers; the latter in festive times ordered luxury items such as Yardley soaps with a scent of lavender or rose, Lindt bars of chocolate, Cadbury chocolate-biscuits, Gruyère, or Tête-de-Maure cheese, and also bottles of Whiskey like Johnny Walker Black Label, or Champagne like Veuve Clicquot.

The other group of employees was comprised of the *commis*. These lived with us as our extended family. They helped mainly in serving the customers at the counters, and performed other chores. They had come from China, as our family did, and worked extremely hard to earn a living. Some to save money to send back home to their families who were left in Meixian. In general, the ultimate goal was to save enough money to buy their own LaBoutique (shop) in a corner of the island. It is to be noted that most considered themselves "travellers" and wanted to return to China one day, just like most Chinese immigrants at the time. We felt compassion and affection for them, for they were a lonely group, most of them so far from their families.

Among the helpers, there were some older relatives of Papa's. For example, Pat Sook Kung who was such a great support to my parents, and who prepared delicious meals for us. And we had our uncles whom we loved. They were Maman's brothers and half-brothers: T.K., her oldest brother, expert in good wines and co-owner of the business, Sankiew and K.K. as well as G. and A. We loved them and they spoiled us. We often sought their company, for the youngest were only a few years older than us. They showed us many things in our young lives. Some of them taught us perseverance, always studying assiduously, striving to finish their studies on their own. Some, like Sankiew, spoiled us by taking us when we were old enough to the cinema called Rio, to see such films as "River of No Return". The most precious thing our uncles (especially K.K. and SanKiew) instilled in us was the love of music (Verdi, Puccini or Gershwin), for they were always intoning opera and operetta arias (like *La Veuve joyeuse, Le Pays du sourire*, and others).

We children of LaBoutique were surrounded by the shop's live-in community and others. For the adults around us who made up our little "clan" also included regular visitors, like CoCo and SaoSao, who were practically part of LaBoutique. They were very close to my parents. Coco used to bring us a special soup made of shank, hock or marrow bone every Saturday morning. We also often saw T.Y.Ti and E., Maman's friends. There was also the constant presence and support of female employees (like Gin), and our maids, who initiated us into the mysteries of adolescence in more ways than one! We participated in the everyday lives of the adults surrounding us, but we children led our own lives as youngsters. We had our own regular visitors: our cousins and our youngest aunt Ah O.

We also had our own school routine. Each morning, before going to school, we had a large breakfast consisting of rice and vegetables stir-fried with a small amount of meat, fish or tofu. Our lunch, carried in a *tente*, was mainly made up of a *pain-maison* with margarine and with a sprinkle of sugar or a drizzle of condensed milk. Sometimes we would have a banana, or some "orange squash" as a treat. We came back from school on time for an early dinner at 4.30 p.m. when we would have the same type of menu as at breakfast, but occasionally we had the luxury of some clear soup, like a watercress or brède *mooroom* (Moringa) broth flavoured with onion. We always ate with a few of the *commis*, and if we were lucky, with one of our parents whenever they could afford the time.

It was only during adolescence that we began to fully realize that our lives were very different from those of our friends. For example, we had no family life, since our parents had to work in the shop the whole day and had no time to eat with us. We were always surrounded by the extended family and employees. Though we loved our uncles, and we had sympathy for the *commis* because they had to work so very hard, far from their own families, we would have liked more privacy, especially when we reached adolescence. There was also this total lack of privacy in terms of our baths. As young girls, for instance, we had to put up with a derelict shed for a bathroom situated in the middle of the courtyard; for each bath we had to place towels or rags at the numerous spots or slits in the bathroom plank walls to protect ourselves from curious eyes!

Therefore, even at a young age, we were fully aware of various challenges. We had to handle a lot of homework as well as help our parents in the shop, at the till or behind the cake counter. The corner behind the cake counter gradually became a private domain to my sister, my four younger brothers and myself. The appropriation of this little universe made us "masters" of our existence in face of some ignorant customers - a very small minority it is true - who mocked us and called us *Ti Sinois*, little Chinky, or the like. Being in this enclave protected us from hurt and safeguarded our pride as children.

We who had not acquired a past yet at our young age were quite precocious and sensitive thanks to our challenging times at LaBoutique: hence we listened with sympathy and compassion when, after their daily chores, Tambi and Salon sat with us to relate *Lé temp Lontan*, the old times, of their ancestors called *Lé temp Margoze*, the bitter old times. These involved the indentureship era, just as Pierre Le Grand had hinted at the time of slavery in his comments. It was much later in life that we were to fully understand the entire scope of what these three characters had told us of the past of their peoples.

There were some good moments to be had at our shop when these men and other helpers in LaBoutique told us stories about *Lougarous*, werewolves. It was our favourite part of the weekend evenings. When we had finished our homework, we sat and listened to their stories of the past, and the tales of ghosts that haunted some of the houses in the town, and the feats of werewolves in remote villages on the island. Very often we would ask for more; at the same time we were reluctant to move around those dark corners of the shop for fear of seeing *Nâmes*, ghosts, or being attacked by those *Lougarous*. Also, we had to avoid walking under the *Pied-Zacques* (jackfruit tree) while crossing the back yard, in case we encountered the evil spirit that might lurk in its shadow at dusk. Our brothers, who for a time lived at the other side of the yard, found it hard because they had no choice but to walk under that tree to reach their sleeping quarters. In walking under some trees, our brothers and others around us could very easily become victims of *mauvaizair* (bad air or spirit), or of a bad curse. In those instances the servants, who descended from African slaves, lit a little charcoal fire, where they threw some camphor: the formation of an "eye" in the embers would be proof that the "evil spell" or "bad spirit" had been made powerless and the victim was safe from harm. Witnessing the gradual shaping of the "eye" in the hot ashes was greatly fascinating to us.

We children believed in all those so-called "superstitions". They were part of our dreams and nightmares, part of our life. Everywhere we went, there was the danger of evil spirits. Each step we took held the risk of bringing us in contact with a ghostly apparition or a werewolf. Because we spent so much time with the maidservants and the employees, the supernatural became part of us. We were frightened but also fascinated by it all.

One big comfort on our way to the "risky" spots was, surprisingly, the backdoor of the tavern with, in its vicinity, the curry block and curry baba utilized to grind the spices, or the wood stove used by Papa to boil ham for customers on special occasions. At dusk, near that back door, it was a relief to see these familiar things, and to hear the constant din from the tavern. The quarrelsome tone of the voices, and sometimes the fracas, were instrumental according to us children in warding off the evil spirits. Therefore, the tavern acted as a protective agent to us during our moments of fear.

It was thus, in this complex and convoluted space of shop and tavern, that our childhood evolved. We spent our young existence with people and helpers who were close to us especially our uncles, but others were strangers who became friends. These crossed our path at the intersection of LaBoutique and the tavern, where we children of Chinese shopkeepers encountered beings of a different milieu. These people brought us the rich dimensions of their lives glimpsed at briefly by us. Our humanity grew abundantly through our connection with these beings. The tavern and the shop continued to exist for many decades, but the shop assistants and such personages as Pierre Le Grand, Tambi and Salon were gone. We often wonder what became of them. We know nothing except that they quietly and gradually disappeared from our lives without us ever noticing. We imperceptibly trod the path to adulthood. Sadly the shop, its tavern, and these beings who had been with us for so many years receded very gently into the past, that past that became with time somewhat distant and foggy, and yet remained an integral part of our innermost selves.

6

CHINESE NEW YEAR

If I were to be asked what the most precious moments of my childhood and adolescence were, I would have to say that they were the Chinese New Year celebrations. From my earliest childhood, I have deeply felt the joy and excitement that prevailed at that time of the year.

Chinese New Year is the most important celebration in the Chinese tradition. It is known as the Spring Festival and dates from the Shang dynasty (17th – 11th centuries B.C.E.). Agricultural in origin, it was initially celebrated with offerings made to the deities and the ancestors. It is celebrated on the first day of the Lunar Calendar (usually at the end of January or the beginning of February). (Chinese New Year History, www.chinesenewyears.info/)

For us children, the atmosphere on this special occasion was filled with the magical warmth and iridescence of festivities unfolding under the humid tropical sun of our small island.

Those days were very special because we were surrounded by our family, and we could feel their affection. Most importantly, we had our parents with us. For usually they worked in the shop and were absent from dawn till night for most of the week, but they spent entire days with us during these special festivities. The whole Chinese community celebrated the New Year over a few days. In this way they made up for missing out on the main feasts of other ethnic groups on the island, that is Christmas and Easter. Chinese shopkeepers could not take part in those celebrations as they had to concentrate on business and capitalize on the fact that those festivals were the busiest times for the shops; when their customers spent more, and when profit was better.

My earliest memories of Chinese New Year celebrations go as far back as the early 1950's, when we moved to the shop in Quatre-Bornes.

My sister and I, with my four little brothers, were between one and seven years of age. How did we start the week-long festivities? It all began with the special dinner held on New Year's Eve (*Nien Samsup Yit*). It was usually a dinner for immediate members of the family but I remember that Maman always invited other members of the family such as her brothers (our *Kiew Kiews*); and the "commis" (shop assistants), some of whom were not closely related to us, but who were considered part of the family unit, as they lived on the premises and shared our daily meals. Ours was a small community modelled on village life back in our ancestral country.

New Year's Eve (the "réveillon") was as important a part of the celebrations as New Year's Day (*Nien Ts'ee Yit*). It was held in the area between the shop and the small house. That space had a roof on one side made of corrugated iron-sheets: this was our dining-room. At the other end, beyond the bedrooms, was the kitchen also patched up with corrugated iron-sheets. The area in between was uncovered and paved with old stones. There, could be found the washing-up areas, one of which had a tap fitted above a big drum. This was used daily by the family (for their morning ablutions, for example).

To begin with, before dinner was served, a small table was placed on one side of the dining room from which offerings were made to the deities and the ancestors as required by tradition. It was a rite Maman set up every year, in which everybody (including all the children) participated by lighting joss sticks and offering them to the ancestors. The offerings on the table consisted of steamed chicken (*B'hak Tsam Keh*), slices of pork, as well as a variety of fruits. Those would be served at dinner and our parents told us that it was important to eat the 'consecrated" food to receive our ancestors' blessings.

We started the rite fairly early as Chinese ate dinner early. From the beginning of the afternoon we could smell the delicious aroma of the special soup that was being prepared (shark's fin soup or another tasty one made with white lichen and mushroom simmered in the stock of a *Rodrigues* chicken). We already anticipated eating the tasty *B'hak Tsam Keh* (boiled in salted water, spring onions and ginger) that had been on the offerings table. It was accompanied by a mustard sauce that would bring tears to our eyes and would make us sneeze. We children were warned about the strength of the mustard sauce but we were determined to have some and had great fun when the mustard hit our throat and nose!

We were surrounded by an abundance of delicacies. We loved the slightly sweet Chinese sausages served with a garlic sauce. One of the dishes served as *hors-d'oeuvres* was the "century-old" preserved eggs that we ate with shredded ginger that had been steeped in vinegar and sugar. The dish the most prized by the adults was the "red pork"; belly pork cooked in wine and red dried fermented rice. We also loved the other pork dish braised with sun dried mustard leaves called *Kon Ham Choy*. There was also Maman's speciality: *Foo Yung*, a soft omelette with Chinese mushrooms, bamboo shoots, minced pork, prawns and spring onions (skillfully cooked on very low heat to produce the perfect consistency). The other dishes were stir-fried chicken and vegetables, steamed fish, *fricassée* of greens with garlic, all eaten with some rice. Many of these were traditional dishes of the Hakka community. The Hakkas created dishes (of preserved vegetables and other ingredients) that would keep well during long journeys: dishes that would withstand long travels. Indeed during their history, the Hakkas had to survive five long historical migrations towards the South - which began as early as year 371 of our era. Those migrations, which happened because of geo-political factors (fall of an Emperor or King, persecutions) or socio-geographical factors (famines), have yielded distinct ways of preserving, cooking and serving foods. Hence, thanks to these old recipes, we Hakkas are still enjoying, to this day, the benefits of our historical migrations!

The table and other parts of the house, the door surrounds, must be covered in red (colour of good luck for the Chinese). There must be a lot of gold everywhere too, to bring prosperity and good fortune. Over the whole house, the lavishness must be in evidence. As children of shopkeepers, we benefited from such an abundance of food only these few days of festivity. Normally in our family we ate simple meals, except for our birthdays, when the birthday boy or girl was entitled to a whole boiled egg (or two if one was lucky). Usually, we had to share an egg with a sibling! The bountiful opulence during the Chinese New Year celebrations had to be on show for the deities, so as to attract multiple blessings from them for the coming year.

Hence, the round table was laden with the delicious dishes prepared by Maman and the cook, and with all sorts of treats. We, the children, sat at a smaller table which was on the other side of the round table but we enjoyed all the dishes too. We were served lemonade as a special treat, and the adults drank a little whisky for a start, and afterwards moved on to beer shandy.

The following day, New Year's Day, we woke up to the sound of fire-crackers that our parents had set off so as to chase away evil spirits and bad luck. This was being done by all the Chinese families on the island. We were used to it and indeed expected the cracking noise that brought good luck on New Year's Day.

On that first day of the New Year, we became vegetarians: a family tradition which served to purify our body and our soul. For the vegetarian dinner, our grandmothers prepared special dishes from their villages in China: fried transparent noodles in a sweet aromatic sauce, or in a spicy sauce served with mustard.

According to Buddhist tradition, on that fasting day it was only at sunset that we could eat meat dishes, left over from the New Year's Eve dinner. This meal was quiet as all the shop assistants had gone to their family or friends, and we were on our own.

Relatives visited each other on this special day and during the next few days. The visits during those days were very important to renew family ties. As most of the Chinese immigrants were shopkeepers, they did not see each other all that often given that they worked more than six days a week and for thirteen-fifteen hours per day. Chinese New Year was one of the rare occasions when the whole family could go out to-gether to meet other relatives. All the members of the community felt close. Even those who were not truly related were considered part of the family. They were close through the solidarity they shared as recent immigrants on the island. More often than not they came unannounced (telephone being rare in those days). There was an open-door policy on those occasions. What happened when a family we visited was not at home? As one might guess, half the community went out visiting other families. To avoid such disappointments, a system of communication had to be devised, or we had to stick to an established routine. We either informed of our visit via a messenger (a relative who had a phone would pass the message on), or we would keep to an already existing arrangement – for example, certain families would be visited on a given day. Where our family was concerned, we stayed at home on the first day, making ourselves available for visits: that fact was well-known to the whole community.

We were impatient to see the relatives and we received them with generous hospitality. Maman served tasty traditional cakes, plates of sweet delicacies (sesame balls called *tian yenneh*/*gato-gingelis,* the sweet gummy *gato-la-cire*), and deep-fried treats (*voo yans* made with taro, tie-shaped *gato-cravattes*, crisps called *cipekes*). Healthy snacks such as sun-flower seeds, watermelon seeds, dried boiled peanuts, were all washed down with steaming-hot Chinese jasmine tea. We welcomed our guests warmly after their long bus journey (some travelled as long as two hours, as they had to cross the island).

It was not long before we heard the clacking noise of the Mah-Jong tiles coming from the dining room. We went over to watch the adults play. They chatted with us in Hakka. If there were children visiting, we played with them. Our parents watched us play and complimented the visitors for the good behaviour of their children (*"An kwai oh!"*). An atmosphere of good humour and kindness prevailed. For us children, the day held special interest as each child received a *foong pow* (a red envelope with money) from the adults on each visit. At the end of the day we very discreetly counted the content of those red envelopes. We felt excited but a little ashamed to show it. Even at our age we instinctively knew that, though it was good to have money to put aside or to give to our parents to buy something later, what counted the most on those days of visits was the human aspect, the deep emotional wealth of family ties.

We would remember the conversations we heard (with half an ear) for many years. Although those conversations sounded fairly important to our young ears, many years would pass before we would understand their full significance.

China always ended up being the focus of conversation. Prevalent was the nostalgia of these people who had been forced to leave a place where they seemed to have been happy; primarily due to financial obligations but for many, it was certainly for political reasons. Civil strife and the Japanese invasion of the land of our ancestors in the 1930's had resulted in the massive diaspora of that particular decade... There is no doubt that nostalgia remained uppermost in the lives of these immigrants who had emotionally never left their homeland, for in the very depth of their beings and in the collective consciousness of their community, remained the epic dream of the "return" to the ancestral home (*tsong T'ong San*), where they would live the rest of their lives!

In the hope of this projected return to the homeland, they were ready to endure much hardship in their new lives in this adopted - and what they took as a "transitory" - place. During those infrequent re-unions, they discussed their life in their shops and how relentlessly they worked the whole week with barely half a day of rest with their family. During those few hours of freedom the men would sometimes meet up with their compatriots in the club of their clan (the *Kwo Neh*) in Port Louis. Women would also escape for a few hours to be with their women friends to help each other, during births, and other occasions.

All the shopkeepers worked very hard for very little profit. Some could hardly survive. They had to pay rent for the premises for, at the beginning, the majority could not afford to buy the property. There were the shop assistants to be housed and provided for. The children were still young but in a few years the secondary school fees would have to be found. Socially, there was the difficulty of adapting to a foreign land. On this multicultural island, there were several cultures to understand and many religions to comprehend: Catholicism, Hinduism, Islam ... not only were there many customs that seemed strange to them, but Creole and one of the Indian languages had to be learned to enable them to do business with the villagers.

With such challenges in their daily lives, one could understand why the Chinese shopkeepers at that period tried to enjoy to the fullest this precious time spent together. The week of festivities normally ended with a picnic or any sort of special outing. For our family, one outing that gave all of us an enormous amount of joy was our annual picnic - the only family outing of the year - at the beach house of one of our customers who had kindly "lent" it to us for the day. It was the last big event of that joyous week. Maman prepared fried chicken marinated in rum or whisky or brandy! It was the best thing on the menu. There were also Indian cakes: *gato-piments* (dhal patties) , *bahjahs* (chickpea fritters), *samosas* (fried wraps)... and a variety of tropical fruits such as bananas, longans, and lychees. On that day, our neighbours, whom we considered as part of our family, joined us on the picnic. We all travelled in the green van which they used for the sale of *brèdes-songes* (taro greens) and watercress. Uncle A. sold vegetables and ran his shop in Port Louis.

The picnic day started early in the morning. We sat on the veranda and in parts of the house we were allowed to use. We played ball in a vast garden we did not own; we splashed in an azure sea that we saw only once a year. We got back home late in the evening, extremely tired after a wonderful day at the beach house of someone we hardly knew!

The week of the Chinese New Year's celebrations was a week of family life as well as a social occasion full of good things: treats from all sides; foods that we only enjoyed for those special festivities; the reciprocated affection between members of a family and between members of our small community. Then, to crown it all, a special moment at the seaside, a whole day filled with the joy that comes from something wonderful; a gift from a stranger kindly granted to us, children of Chinese shopkeepers. That was the magic with which our week of celebrations ended!

7

The "Board" at Quatre-Bornes

The town of Quatre Bornes also known as *La Ville des Fleurs* (The City of Flowers) is located in the district of Plaines Wilhems named after Wilhem Leicknig who had settled in the region in 1721. It is generally believed that the name "Quatre-Bornes" derives from the "four boundary stones" (*"quatre bornes"*) that bordered the estates of Palma, Bassin, Trianon and Beau Séjour. But according to some historians, the name comes from a court litigation in 1761 between two estate owners who fought about the limits of their properties and "four boundary markers" ("le cas des quatre bornes"). At the time, Quatre-Bornes was shown on maps of the island as only a forest. It was gradually colonized during the next several decades. During the British rule, as early as in 1864, it had the benefit of a railway system linking it to several towns and villages, but it was proclaimed a "village" only in 1890, and a "town" later in 1896. (The Municipal Council of Quatre-Bornes: "History of Quatre-Bornes", www.qb.mu)

The municipal building of Quatre-Bornes was known to the inhabitants of the town as the "Board". The term was probably adopted from the inception of the town because the "board" of deputies or commissioners administered the region from that building. It was a wooden construction built around 1930 in the British colonial style. It was to be demolished after the devastation caused by Cyclone Carol in 1960, and replaced a few years later by a modern edifice.

However, as youngsters growing up in the 1950's, we benefited fully from the old Board. Every Saturday evening, we children of local shopkeepers and workers from impoverished middle-class families made our way to the "Hotel de Ville de Quatre-Bornes", our townhall known in Creole as the "*Board-Kat-Born*". We were usually with our cousins E., E. and M., and other friends. Some adults like Gin, Fidou and E. kindly accompanied us. It was our weekly habit to converge to the Board to watch whatever wedding might be taking place there. It was a place renowned for its beautiful spacious hall and vast dancing floor prized by the inhabitants of our small island.

Therefore, in the 1950's, the early years of our childhood, we would often be seen at the wooden colonial building. It was fronted by very large glazed bay windows which made it possible for us to watch the dancing "from the wings" of the stage so to speak: from there, actors and dancers kindly let us watch their show. We got as near to the glass panes as possible, observing for hours, greedy for the show which we could enjoy for free.

There we watched, unfolding in front of us on that stage, a social spectacle or rather, a "social comedy". We, children of a less privileged milieu, saw full of elation the guests arriving in their magnificent automobiles. The ladies wore their ball gowns made of taffeta, satin or Crêpe de Chine. The young girls were dressed in silk or tulle. The dresses were usually fashioned in a princess line with flared skirts, in bright or pastel colours that dazzled us. The fabric would be plain or patterned but always of the finest material. We could not stop admiring them. Not even in our dreams would we have dared to wear these extraordinary gowns!

Also, we had the opportunity of observing various social circles present at those receptions. There, we looked at the customers we served at LaBoutique (our family business) in a different light. We saw who were the "wallflowers", that is the girls who throughout the evening did not move from their chairs for lack of invitation from the gentlemen. We discovered who were the best dancers in the diverse social groups on the island - and indeed who were the most popular young ladies in town.

It was therefore an enjoyable show on several levels, but it was the dances that fascinated us the most: waltzes, Quadrilles, and Lancers. The ball usually opened with the bride and groom dancing the Viennese Waltz. We saw them gliding gracefully across the shiny floor. The bridesmaids and best men soon joined them. I think that my love for the waltz started then. The mellifluous music was magical to our ears, a sweet wave of comfort and joy. It was always the same dance band (The Police Band directed by Maestro Wan) performing at those social events of the well-to-do social strata. We went to see those weddings not only to admire the dancers but also to listen to the best music to be had on the island.

We would arrive around 7.00 p.m. and would remain until past 9.00 p.m. if it was the summertime. At a certain point of the evening we would hurry to get back home, prompted by the fear of Papa's anger. In the summer it was still pleasant outdoors at 9.00 p.m. but in the winter it was a different thing altogether. If the weddings took place in the rainy season, we did not stay long because of the wind and rain that made us feel chilled.

Visits to the Board were not limited to Saturdays for the weddings. We would also take a walk there on Sundays during the day for fresh air, exercise and entertainment. We loved strolling along the flowerbeds and well kept lawns. On one of those outings, our brother B. who was running by the edge of the fishpond, fell in the greenish water. We fished him out after a bit of a struggle. He was completely drenched and we could see his flip-flops floating among the fishes and frogs. All the way home, he was shaking, and slimy green water was dripping from him. He was also covered in moss and what looked like small snail-like creatures. The continuous shivering was due to the chill but a great part of it was probably brought on by the thought of the hiding that awaited him. We knew that Papa would not accept his excuses. He would say that if B. had fallen into the pond, it was because of sheer carelessness!

For several years before "the pond" incident, visiting the Board on a summer afternoon or evening was a ritual that had shaped our young lives. Suffice to say that those visits to the Board were far less frequent following the "B.-fell-in-the-pond" incident.

Then again, after having been at the centre stage of our lives for so long, the wooden building of the Board had to be demolished and rebuilt after Cyclone Carol. Funds were allocated to replace it with a modern structure modelled, they said at the time, after the United Nations building in New York (no doubt a vastly exaggerated statement which we were too patriotic to dispute then)! The new building opened its door in 1964. Naturally the enormous glazed windows were gone, depriving us of the pleasure of enjoying the social functions held there. The cemented construction afforded no view of the dancing and the thick walls made it hard to hear the band's charming music. Our visits there stopped. It may also be that we were growing into adolescents who needed more sophisticated ways of "passing the time" (i.e. at matinées and parties).

As adults, we can still feel the delight of our visits to the Board when we drive in that part of town during each trip back home. These moments remain among our sweetest memories. We think of those fascinating periods of our childhood when under the warm sky of our island, we were able to glimpse a world of dream and luxury within the frames of those bay windows. We were fortunate to experience albeit briefly through those magical apertures, the life of the privileged of the island. We developed within ourselves a certain wisdom that would last us a lifetime thanks to those moments; for from those spectacles at *Board-Kat-Born* we derived the knowledge that despite all difficulties, life could sometimes carry its share of joy and pleasure!

8

OUR ANNUAL PICNIC

The only big outing we shopkeepers' children on the island had during the year was our Chinese New Year's outing, that is, the day-picnic we as a family undertook annually.

Our parents had no holiday other than the few days they took off, away from LaBoutique (our grocery store), on the occasion of the Chinese New Year. For them, Christmas and New Year celebrations were far from being days of festivities: on the whole, they had to work harder on these two occasions when the other communities increased their grocery purchases, the wealthier ones buying things like the special boiled ham Papa cooked on a wood fire in a lemon-grass brine, the Lindt chocolates wrapped in special festive boxes, and the Veuve Clicquot Champagne.

Therefore it was only in the week around Chinese New Year that my parents allowed themselves some time off and celebrated. They then got to relax and enjoy some festivity. Chinese New Year was extremely special since they considered themselves more Chinese than Mauritian.

It was in the early 1950's. The Chinese immigrants on the island were still small in number, and very close-knit. At that time, the extended family members and even members of the community who were not blood relations considered themselves as *Tsee Ka Nien* (part of the same family). During the week of Chinese New Year, they usually paid a visit to each other. On these visits, they enjoyed special dishes, Chinese tea and festive cakes. They also played Mah-Jong during long hours. Since most of them were shopkeepers like my parents, this was the only occasion when they could spend a number of hours together in a spirit of relaxation and celebration. We children enjoyed all this festivity. We also loved the fact that we did not have to help in the shop, at the cash till, or behind the cake counter, that corner which we had made ours, and where we took shelter from the prejudice of some of the customers – albeit rare – who called us "little Chineys".

During the celebrations, we liked the treats (especially the Foong Pows - red money packages!), the dinners, and the service for the ancestors under the tropical sky of our little island. However, one of the events we most enjoyed in that festive period was our annual picnic at the seaside. It was the only opportunity for us to go out together as a family. After the big meal which the cook and my mother had prepared for *Nien SamSupYit* (New Year's eve), we would begin to get ready for the major event of the week: our annual picnic at the villa (*campement*) of Madame X who was one of our customers. Every year, she graciously agreed to "lend" us for one day her *campement* at Rivière Noire.

Madame X was of the so-called "White" population of the island referred to as "les Blancs" or Franco-Mauritians, descendants of the French colonizers of the island. They colonized Mauritius after the Portuguese and Dutch abandoned the island, after Mahé de Labourdonnais began as of 1735 his remarkable development of Isle de France (old name for Mauritius). These French settlers set up sugarcane plantations, then imported in great numbers slaves from Africa and Madagascar to work for them. By 1767, the Whites numbered only 2,000; the slaves serving them on the plantations and elsewhere outumbered them by more than 16,000 (Fillion, Jean-Michel: 1989). It was from this juxtaposition of cultures that the Creole language evolved. At the time, society condoned slavery and gave almost absolute power to plantation owners, allowing them to abuse and mistreat their slaves. However, in spite of this cruel system, there were good and kind masters even then, to compensate for the cruelty of the others. As we witnessed in our youth, the descendants of these powerful masters did show kindness to us. And as our parents taught us, we should not stereotype any given group despite a very dark past. Moreover, after almost two centuries, there has been drastic social change on the island where nowadays power is shared more democratically than in those remote times.

In our childhood, we were deprived of a car for the longest time. We had to take a taxi to reach the villa at the seaside: a journey of about 45 minutes. However, after AmeeTi became engaged to Uncle A., it was in his dark-green van that we travelled. AmeeTi and her mother PakPak had been our nextdoor neighbours for years. We considered them as family, though we were not blood relations.

In that big green van, the adults loaded all the children who fortunately at the time were still very young and thin. The excitement was at its paroxysm: we sang cheerful songs (*Au clair de la Lune*, *Frère Jacques*, *A la Claire Fontaine*), and we laughed loudly without being scolded. Life was wonderful. Nothing could jeopardize the next few hours of bliss and freedom we thought we were entitled to.

The trip to Rivière Noire was not a lengthy one, but for people who never travelled in a car, it seemed long and endless, especially when the van was packed to the brim, and the summer heat made it worse for some of us without the benefit of a window at the back. After about 30 minutes, Pak-Pak falling half asleep would ask the driver if we were nearly there: "*Sofia, Sofia, KeKe Von La Miéh, hangkor loiing?*" She spoke Creole mixed with Chinese, with an oriental tone and accent. We children giggled - being careful, out of respect for her age, not to laugh at her too loudly!

We reached the *campement* soon enough. It was a large bungalow right on the beach, rustic and elegant. We had to cross the imposing lounge to reach the open veranda. We were puzzled by the deer heads on the walls – memorabilia of past hunts. And we were in awe of the old-silver framed family photos of the ancestors. The scent emanating from the house as soon as our father opened the side door was that of old teak or mahogany furniture that had been waxed and polished recently. A whiff of mustiness permeated the air for the initial few seconds. Beside the nice smell of polished wood, there was the aroma of the perfumed soaps in the bathroom: all that reflected the comfort and luxury of a world foreign to us shopkeepers' children.

The chairs in the living room were padded with cushions. The wicker sofas that gave the villa a cheery and tropical character were moved to the veranda for the day, so we could sit and enjoy the full panorama of the garden in the front, and the beach and sea further ahead. We enjoyed being for once a real family, being with our parents almost all day without being interrupted by the customers! Maman was smiling, and Papa more relaxed than usual.

Generally, it would not rain on our special day. However, if we had a summer sprinkle, we would eat in the veranda or even in the kitchen.

The morning of that day, mother usually prepared deep fried or roasted chicken done in a rotisserie, which she kept in a big *catora* (aluminum covered cylinder). In other containers were packed a variety of treats prepared by our elders mainly for the festivities. These included *gato-la cire* (a sweet cake), *tien yieneh* (fried sesame seed balls), and other fried delicacies like *gato-cravattes* (tie-shaped snacks). As a snack, the adults liked to munch gluttonously on roasted watermelon seeds, which they split with their teeth with great skill. The bread for lunch was *Pains-Maison*, in which we inserted the chicken, garnished with some crispy lettuce and homemade mayonnaise. Maman oftentimes made a *Moun Fan* (a sort of Chinese *pilau* rice) with plenty of Chinese sausages and mushrooms. And this, we enjoyed for our early supper before leaving the *campement*. On that day, we were allowed soft drinks (Pepsi, Coca and Fanta).

I remember that the reality of spending several hours in a luxurious environment was almost too overwhelming to bear lightly. Compared to our minute room behind the shop, where we spent hours cooped up, all six of us in a restrained space, this villa with its garden and sea view was paradise!

What did we play with at the villa? Did we own a ball? Or did we just sit there, relaxed and content, just like grown-ups in full contemplation of the sea? Just being there was the greatest of treats! The adults just sat replete with contentment, sitting on the chairs on the veranda or on the lawn on *nattes* (straw rugs), chatting quietly and eating all the goodies. I remember that we children enjoyed taking walks or running after a hen in the big garden, and picking the fruit of the red and golden leafed *Badamier* tree at the edge of the garden, where it formed an angle with the beach. We would crush these fruits with stones to extract the nuts from within and eat them. We also enjoyed digging the sand, looking for beach *tek-teks* (clams): people on the island prize these for their sweet taste, especially when simmered in a broth and eaten with rice. The same went for small crustaceans called "bigorneaux" which we liked to collect from the sides of big boulders in the shallow clear water. We used to fight in the water as we threw our ball at each other to splash the water all over our faces. We would tread the turquoise sea to collect the ball. In this secluded corner of the infinite sea, in that great emerald ocean, we children were not afraid to imitate swimmers whom we saw in the deeper water. In the shallow limpid water, we tried to float ("faire la planche"), and to do some diving with our eyes open, all this in our undershirt and little trunks, for at one point when we were very young, we owned no swimming suits!

At the end of the day, soothing in its calm and peaceful atmosphere, the sky above the horizon beckoned us on the beach. There was the gold and the fire of the setting sun to contemplate; there was the honey and silver of the sea to capture. There was also the caressing sea breeze to feel. In this firmament foreign to us, we would slowly inhale all the soothing air. We had come to realize, especially when we reached a certain age, that we had to optimize, both sensually and emotionally, that rare treat which was bestowed upon us. There were all the pleasures of the day to encapsulate in our memory so we could keep them for a whole year, until our return in that corner of Rivière Noire the following Chinese New Year!

In the van, in the hours between dusk and night, we would be rocked by the movement of the vehicle, humming something nostalgic, like "*Mo Passer la Rivière Tanier*" to comfort ourselves. The sweet memories of that day, stashed away in a precious little nook, would prepare us for the days ahead, as a solace in life's challenges. Those remembrances would give us the strength and vitality to move on, in our simple and challenging lives as "zenfants" LaBoutique. Young as we were, we knew that we had to be grateful. Grateful to that family of "Blancs" who had lent their *campement* to us whom they hardly knew. They had been kind, we thought, to share with us during an entire day a small parcel of their luxurious universe!

9

ALFRED THE SHOEMAKER

There is no doubt that he puzzled us and we were not too sure why. He had a distinctive smell: a mixture of body odour and leather. After all, he worked with leather for his repairs all day long. There was also his size: he was at least six feet tall and heavily built. His hair was half frizzy and half curly. It looked most of the time like a thick ball of wool resting on his head, through which no comb had passed for donkey's years.

It could not have been his rugged appearance that was at the root of this questioning we had. Nor was it his work. During the past couple of years, we had watched him in his shoemaker routine. We liked to observe how he rubbed wax along the length of a few strands of shoe-sewing thread and rolled them together between both palms to make them stronger and weatherproof. He would then pass the string through big needles, or using an awl, he would push it through holes made in the sole and upper part of the shoe. We helped him with some of his tasks, and we were thrilled when he finished refurbishing the whole shoe. However, before this could be achieved, he would have had to trace the shape of the foot onto the leather and cut it out roughly; then cut the contour very precisely with a very sharp knife, using a pattern and producing the perfect shape. He would go through this whole process for each shoe. The final task was to polish the repaired shoes and brush them with his polishing tools until they shone in the dim light of the workshop. He finished the task with great satisfaction, and we shared his pride.

There was hardly room to move in his workshop due to the low seats, the old pedal sewing machine and his stout legs. He arrived at around 6.00 o'clock in the morning, even before our shop opened. He entered his workshop through the front door. This was barely high enough to allow him into the tiny space. The sort of lean-to had a sloping roof that was attached to the shop (our family business). In a dilapidated state, it was enhanced by a small window that was roughly cut out of the facade on one side of the door. The shack was constructed with wood from some crates and a few panels of rusty iron sheets that patched the damages caused by several cyclones. It leaned to one side, as if it was in constant danger of collapsing. Lit by a paraffin lamp when there was no electricity after the cyclones, it was like something out of a fairy tale. The dimly lit window attracted us, just as in tales of witches and wolves the far-away light in the little window attracts children lost in the big dark forest.

We accessed the workshop from the back entrance which we could reach through a side alley from our dining-room. There, in this room that was in fact a large area partly exposed to the elements, a side door faced Alfred's shed.

That shack was on the side of the shop compound opposite that wing occupied by Pak-Pak and Ah Mee Ti, our neighbours. And beyond that wing, across the jackfruit tree alley, was the rented accommodation for the shop assistants. There, our younger brothers B. and L. would move to later on. When the latter reached their teenage years, our parents felt that the older boys had to move out of our small room where all six children had been living.

At the time, that is when we were around five or six years of age, as we were not threatened by any obvious danger, we were allowed to go to the various parts of the property. Most days, we were quite free to make our way to Alfred's workshop, spending more time there during the long holidays and on the weekends.

He welcomed us, with his customary silence. At times he had other visitors: one of these was Robert, the local barber, whose hair was even more dishevelled than Alfred's. However, the cobbler was on his own most of the time, working with his thread and awl, his shoe soles, his shoe polish. For months on end, it was the usual visit, the usual routine.

However, one day I started to feel a certain unease around Alfred. It began when I suddenly realized that he was holding me by the waist and stroking my small legs! Something rang the alarm in me but as a young child, I could not understand exactly why. When it happened a second time, my instinct as a young child triggered a heightened state of alarm.

The whole thing had happened insidiously enough with movements that were hesitant at first then more audacious. That second time, I became fully aware of a serious menace. It did not take me long to know that something unsavoury, of direct concern to me, had taken place in that workshop. Hence I stopped going to the small shed, a place where I was supposedly safe from the dangers of the outside world.

For many years, when I saw Alfred on the street, near the bank or the market, I lowered my eyes pretending that I had not seen him. I felt ashamed as if I was the one who had done something wrong.

Years later when I went back home to the island, I told myself that I was not the guilty party, and I allowed myself to think that I should confront him one day. Time passed and as an adult I talked to my sister. It seems that she too had been subjected to the same treatment from the hands of that man whom we had considered a friend.

As time elapsed, we no longer saw Alfred the shoemaker near the market. He had retired from the world as quietly as he had lived, no doubt in seclusion and in silent guilt of his perversion.

10

AMEE TI AND PAK-PAK

There were just the two of them. Mother and daughter. One elderly, the other almost middle-aged.

It was at the beginning of the 1950's. Pak-Pak had come from China almost twenty years earlier (in the 1930's) and Amee Ti had already adopted the Mauritian mentality, culture and language. She spoke Creole, like everyone on our small island, whilst her mother, as most of the Chinese immigrants of her generation, only spoke Chinese, with a few words of Creole.

Amee Ti was a dressmaker. At least that was what occupied her time when she had some work. The room they rented was to the north of the building where our shop was. Their lodging was divided in two parts: the area where they slept, and the space where they worked. The two sections were kept separate by a curtain of faded yellow fabric printed with flowers that were barely visible. Their bedroom was a cramped space that contained a large iron bed that they shared. It had neither window nor skylight. At the other side was what could barely pass for a workroom, a generous description indeed for the corner where the dressmaker kept her foot-operated Singer sewing machine. It was rusty and old, and would have been bought second-hand, quite possibly from the tailor nearby. This part of the room had a small window fitted with three anti-burglar bars. It led to the kitchen-cum-bathroom made of somewhat rusty metal sheets with holes and slits in them. This makeshift annex overlooked the backyard that clients had to cross when they came to see Amee Ti, either to order new dresses or for fittings.

At a lower level, a few steps from this door, was a small compound that consisted of a few chicken coops made of assembled planks from wooden crates. Pak-Pak fed her hens morning and night. She was usually dressed in her worn black cotton *Sam Foo* (Chinese costume). She talked to her hens in Chinese while feeding them maize, followed by scraps of bread, as if they were adored children who had to be coaxed with soft words to encourage them to eat (*S'it Nah. An Voy!*). Her wrinkled face, her thin hands deformed by arthritis, presented a figure who had lived through too much sadness, poverty and hardship. However, the kindness and sweetness glimmering in her eyes brought much comfort and warmth to our hearts, in our simple lives as children of shopkeepers.

We liked to watch her perform her chores. Like all the women of her generation, she sewed Chinese cotton slippers and *chaussons*. She made these with much dexterity and expertise. We would also observe her while she prepared supper. We will never forget the rice broth she used to make. After the rice had been cooked, she poured the water in a big bowl and left the rice in the pan to keep warm. She then added a little salt to the boiling rice water, and a handful of pickled vegetable if she had any, and served this as a broth. The frugal meal of rice and vegetables (stir-fried with a little meat) was made more digestible by the hot broth.

We children also remember the beverage she made in the evening. She would boil watered down milk to which she added a spoonful of drinking chocolate. Leftover cooked rice would be added to the milky drink to stave off hunger before going to bed. In her generosity she invited us to savour her hot drink. We did not realize that she was poorer than us. In all innocence we accepted to share her little supper, making her portion even smaller. To us the piping hot concoction was delicious, if somewhat unusual.

Amee Ti was busy in her workroom almost all day to earn a living. She was particularly busy when there was a wedding, and during festivities such as Easter and the New Year. We liked watching her make the dresses, alterations and repairs she was assigned to do. She gave us scraps of material that we utilized to make dolls' skirts. She taught us how to tack and how to gather the skirt on a dress. In those days, as we did not have a television, we enjoyed spending time with our neighbours. Our life was thus filled with moments shared with two people who would have remained unknown to us under other circumstances, but who had become close and dear to us in the special context of the LaBoutique (our shop).

The shop was in fact next to the sewing room that shared a wall with our tavern. When we were with our neighbours on the weekends, we often heard the arguments of the people drinking in the tavern. The noise started around eleven in the morning and lasted usually until seven in the evening; the intensity and level of noise increased steadily as more and more alcohol was consumed.

For a few years, our routine at Amee Ti's did not change. We sat near her, watched her perform her sewing tasks, and chatted with her while we attempted to make miniature clothes. She talked to us as a big sister would, rather than as an aunt. To our mind, she was very trendy: she wore fashionable clothes and had her hair permed. She was fairly good-looking, but had to watch her weight. She wore lipstick when going out and liked to accessorize her patent shoes with small squarish leather handbags that were so popular in the 1950's. At the mature age of nearly thirty, she had a generous figure and an open and direct personality.

One fine Sunday, we were told that we could not visit Amee Ti. We had to leave her alone as she was expecting a visitor. We very quickly discovered (by peeping through the gaps in the kitchen wall) that the visitor was a gentleman. He wore a smart grey suit with a hat to match. Slim compared to our neighbour, he had a tanned skin and distinguished features. During the week, we overheard conversations between our parents and Pak-Pak: the gentleman liked Amee Ti and had asked for her hand in marriage.

When we saw our neighbour a few days later, she looked a bit out of sorts. As children, we could not ask her any questions. We followed the development of events as in a romantic magazine. Even if she did not agree with the arrangements, she was in no position to refuse the offer. This is what our parents thought. Amee Ti was thirty and was already considered a spinster by society. Why did she not like the gentleman? Well, it would appear that he was through and through Chinese in mentality, whereas she was "westernized". She could speak Creole and French. Although she spoke Chinese to her mother, she no longer considered herself to be a "Chinese from China". Finally, as we understood from all the snippets of conversations, she had no choice in the matter. Either she married and settled down in Port Louis at the shop the gentleman owned and take her mother with her, or she and her mother languished all their lives, more or less in poverty, in this too quiet corner of Quatre-Bornes...

She married Tonton A. after a courtship of a few months. Pak-Pak settled with the newly weds in the capital city. We were often invited to stay there during the long school holidays (we would stay a few days at a time). Our brothers B. and L. were very happy to accompany Tonton A. on his business rounds to his watercress and *brèdes-songes* (taro greens) cultivations in some deep valley in the countryside. Later on, our youngest brothers J. and E. would go with them. We spent time with Amee Ti and Pak-Pak in the shop or in the back yard. The property where the shop was located was spacious. It held a great charm for us as the kitchen opened onto a very large and tidy garden with a *maçon* tree and other tropical fruit trees (Mangoes, Lychees, Longans, Tamarind). We ate plenty of all the different fruits with chillied salt. In that big space, we helped Pak-Pak "clean" rice by thrashing it in a large shallow round wicker tray (*vanne*), and we also liked to chase her hens. She seemed happy there, in that yard, feeding her hens and doing the cooking. Amee Ti and her husband looked after the shop. They sold rice and other basic commodities to the local community. They rented comics and romance magazines out to their customers. We were allowed to read those when we became adolescents.

A few years after their marriage they had two children. A girl came first closely followed by a boy. Pak-Pak ended her days in peace and contentment.

Over the years, we spent many happy holidays with our ex-neighbour and her family. Our visits decreased gradually as we grew older and found other interests. However, we maintained contact by telephone and regular visits, especially for the Chinese New Year.

Some years passed without anything of great interest. We were finishing our studies and we were preparing ourselves to face the big wide world. One fine day we heard that Amee Ti had become mentally ill. We heard that she had suffered a change of personality: she would verbally abuse everyone and it became more and more serious; so much so that, after a few years, her family had to take her to a "convent", a place where mentally challenged people, who could not be looked after at home, ended their days.

As we grew older, we did wonder if it was schizophrenia or the depressive illness of someone who was living an unhappy life? And yet, all those years, she had seemed to us content enough: she had a good husband and good children, as well as a supportive mother until her adulthood. Or maybe we were mistaken: unbeknownst to us, she might have felt in a prison from which she was subconsciously trying to escape? After all, her destiny was forged by social and economic constraints! How often had she had the luxury of doing what she truly wanted to do, loved whom she wanted and gone where she wanted? These questions will remain unanswered.

It was a very sad day when we heard that Amee Ti was dying. She died after a brief period in a coma. She was perhaps in her forties. All this seems to have happened a long time ago, but she still holds a very special place in our hearts and our childhood memories. Whereas Pak-Pak will always be remembered for her sweetness, Amee Ti will be remembered as someone who loved and spoiled us when we needed it. We truly loved her and respected her as a big sister.

11

Alley of the Jackfruit Tree

The Jackfruit Tree Alley ran between LaBoutique (our shop) and the rooms where the Simonier family lived. We called the lane *L'Allée Pied-Zaques* (Jackfruit Tree Alley) because most of it enjoyed the shade of an immense century-old jackfruit tree. It was a giant tree, about 12 meters tall. This species generally produces enormous fruits (*fruits-Zaques*) of a green-yellowish colour, anywhere from 50 to 75 centimetres in length.

All people on our small island, young and old alike, are fond of this fruit in its diverse usage. If the fruit is unripe, it is used to make delicious curries. If the fruit has reached full ripeness, it is served as a sweet and succulent desert. Also, the abundant pods constituting the fruit contain big seeds (*LaGrains-Zaques*) of oblong shape, about three to four centimetres in diameter – potato-like in consistency. These big seeds can be boiled and used as a most satisfying snack for afternoon tea. In fact, on account of its sheer size, whenever a jackfruit is "opened", the family has to share it with friends and neighbours. There is this general belief that a *fruit-Zaques* is impressive enough, both in size and in substance, to feed a whole village!

The Alley at the one end away from the street led into the large property of the Beau-Séjour family. It is undoubtedly human to want to know how others from a different social class live. For instance, did we not often see Mario Beau-Séjour peek through the narrow gaps in the bamboo hedge to watch us in our various activities when we were playing games? Usually, we tried to ignore his presence, except perhaps for some brief exchanges like "Hello", "Salam" ... He was after all a young boy who seemed nice enough when we encountered him on the streets in the neighbourhood. He probably just wanted to know what we, the shopkeepers' children (inferior and poor from his perspective) were up to in that alley! In truth, did we not ourselves frequently peek through these same slits in the hedge to watch his family going into their spacious house or going out in their big British car? Did we not surreptitiously observe guests joining them for a certain festivity, or watch the gardeners working in the lush garden! We could not refrain from being curious about the other side of the hedge for, through that narrow opening in the bamboo at the end of the Alley, we could have a glimpse of another world - so luxurious and so different from ours!

Indeed, whenever we watched the Beau-Séjours go into their big car, it occurred to us even at our young age that we were not of the same class. Whenever we observed the lifestyle of these neighbours and that of our clients at the shop, our young instinct told us that we must be quite "poor" compared to them. For they bought all sorts of things from the shop, these privileged people from the immense sugar plantations and the huge colonial houses with their vast gardens along the country roads of Quatre-Bornes, Beau-Bassin or Curepipe.

That elite class purchased what we could not afford. For special celebrations, they ordered Ham-on-the bone that Papa and his team boiled in lemon-grass and spices on a big wood stove at the back of the shop; *Black label* whisky; *Veuve Clicquot* champagne; all manner of imported tinned foods such as "Champignons de Paris", asparagus and pears; delicacies such as crystallized fruit, Australian butter, Edam cheese, chocolates from Switzerland (*Lindt*); and fine French Wines (*Château Lafite*). They often ordered dainty ham and mustard sandwiches for their parties. Our parents prepared those. These customers would send their grocery lists to the shop or give us the list over the telephone. If they did not collect the groceries, the "boys" on their bicycles would deliver these to their house. They would purchase the goods on credit, listing them in the "little red book", and they would settle the bill at the end of the month. There were a few who never settled their bills in full and that left Papa with debts that he had to settle with the wholesalers in Port-Louis. Mario Beau-Séjour undoubtedly belonged to this well-to-do social class. Whilst we did not have direct access to the lifestyle of "the rich", we most certainly had the opportunity, however obliquely, to observe through the shop and through the Alley, a class of people who led a life substantially remote from ours!

In sharp contrast to this elite universe, at the other end of the Alley, a little closer to the road and partly sheltered by the refreshing shade of the jackfruit tree, was to be found the small world of Mr Jean Simonier and his family.

Their apartment was in a building that housed some workshops and a shop. In the front, facing Royal Road (later called St. Jean Road) were three workrooms: that of Mr Jean, a tailor by trade; that of Mr Ramaine, a handyman and jack of all trades; and that of Mr Robert, our local barber. At the intersection of Route Royale and the road leading to St. Rosaire church was the luxury shop called "Vues-Modernes".

The Simoniers lived behind that commercial part of the building. Through our interaction with them, we were exposed to yet another culture, another cuisine.

Being in the lane allowed us to often "visit" the Simonier family (Ma-Rose, Marie and their younger brothers) - usually for a few minutes, just before their meal times. They used tin or enamel plates (very exotic in our view) containing a little rice on which some watercress soup had been ladled. In one corner of the plate, there was a small amount of *chatini* (chutney). The meal was enhanced by a piece of fried salted fish. At times, a lentil or dhal soup replaced the watercress soup. During the summer, in the heat of our tropical island, they often ate on the stone steps leading to their apartment. But in the winter, the family had their meals in the small kitchen, and they ate with such good appetite! Mr Jean joined them later when he had closed his shop. While playing in the Alley, we could smell the onions and garlic frying. The aroma made us a little hungry since we had eaten our dinner at 4.00 p.m. We did not go too near their kitchen during the meal as we felt it would be rude to do so. Occasionally Mrs Jean would nicely call us over to share some of the soup, but we thanked her politely and we kept away, as children instinctively have a sense of dignity towards themselves and others.

We of Chinese tradition had a different lifestyle, another cuisine. We usually ate vegetables stir-fried with a bit of meat with our rice. Therefore, seeing the meals of the Simonier family was to gradually become much more appreciative of the aromas of the Creole cuisine. We were hardly aware that theirs were simple meals for ordinary people whose daily diet, just like the majority of families on the island, consisted of very little meat.

Their kitchen was a small lean-to outside the apartment. In fact, it was the most run-down part of the building. The walls were made of rusty iron sheets. The damaged parts had been repaired with bits from "drums". This lean-to and other parts of the building had been damaged by a great number of cyclones. (Later in 1960, the kitchen would be almost completely destroyed by Cyclone Carol).

A fence made of old iron-sheets had originally separated the yard of the Simoniers from the lane. As this fence was gradually destroyed by various cyclones, the two plots of land eventually merged into an indeterminate derelict area where the children of both families played. Although in that area the air circulation was rather poor, for us it was the "open air" compared to the stifling air in our small maisonette. For us in LaBoutique, we had two bedrooms to sleep six - or eight children, that is, when our youngest aunt A. or little cousins T-M. and Ti-M. from Rodrigues and from Rose-Hill came to stay on the holidays! We experienced an enormous pleasure playing in the shade of the jackfruit tree. For us it was the freedom of open space.

Generally, we were allowed to play in the Alley for a longer period of the day on the weekends or during the long holidays. The Simoniers' older children joined us whenever they could. Oftentimes, we played near the road. But there, the sun was so strong that we had to move down the lane to seek the comforting shade of the big jackfruit tree. We usually played a multitude of games in the hide-and-seek style; or we simply raced along the Alley for a bet (*pariaze-galouper*). We played the *LaMarelle*, a game requiring a flat area. Therefore, on an even spot in the lane, we traced some squares in the dirt and pushed a small stone from square to square, hopping about on one foot. We also enjoyed the "elastic game" that involved throwing elastic bands in the squares or circles drawn in the ground with a chalk or stick. We also organized exciting ball games, hitting each other with those soft balls, or running like mad in order not to be "caught".

There is no doubt that this lane, narrow and seemingly of such little importance, afforded my brothers, my sister and myself a glimpse of the different worlds, to us so full of mystery, of people on 'the other sides of the tract" as it were, either richer than us - or poorer than us.

In the mid 1950's, when we got a little older, we decided that we would learn to ride a bicycle. Maman had an old bicycle (was it a Raleigh?) we could practise on. We took turns to ride it, hardly managing to ride astride, and unable to reach the saddle; one foot still on the ground to gain momentum. My little brothers, my sister and I must have been between three and twelve years old. We helped our siblings by pushing the bike, especially the younger ones. We started at the top of the lane that was near the main road. Then we cycled downhill towards the jackfruit tree. The gentle slope made it possible for us to learn to pedal; we tried not to lose our balance. The true challenge came when we had to cycle uphill but that became less difficult with practice and after a few falls. We came out of those "challenges" with numerous scratches, as the ground was hard and pebbly. We felt triumphant when we finally succeeded: Maman's bicycle was our racehorse – and what an old good racehorse it was, taking such abuse from us kids!

One day the play area provided by the Alley was drastically reduced, the space having to be shared with Papa's new van. The lane belonged to our family in theory, since we rented out the whole complex where the shop was located. So our father had the right to park his vehicle there. From then on, we had to compete with the green Gazelle for space. We found it difficult to ride the bicycle when the van was parked there; we had to ride around it, and the lack of space quickly discouraged us. We could not wait to practise riding the bike on the road in the coming years.

Hence, the Jackfruit Tree Alley, after many years of being used by the children as their exclusive kingdom, became Papa's property and the family garage. By and by, the children grew into secondary school teenagers who no longer played in the lane. In time, we only used it on our way home from school when the shop was closed (on Wednesday and Sunday afternoons). In those years, we rarely saw the Simoniers. Gradually, the lane became deserted. An empty space where there were no activities, laughter or the sound of bicycle wheels.

One day during my adolescent years I went looking for Ma-Rose and Marie to say a little "hello", only to be told that the family had moved. We had never said goodbye. That was the price we paid after a long silence on both sides. Time took over our easy-going lives as children, and the harsher reality of our journey as adolescents and young adults gradually and surreptitiously superseded those innocent and unforgettable moments of our tender age.

No doubt, the Alley played an important role in our lives. It helped us become aware of our "place" in society. Growing up and playing in that lane, we began to become conscious that, being children of Chinese shopkeepers, we had a different lifestyle from the Beau-Séjours and the Simoniers: these families were of different cultures – at two ends of a social spectrum; and we were somewhere in the middle. The lane thus became the intersecting space of three social backgrounds, where the children acted as some sort of pawns on a checkerboard, interacting with each other in a number of ways, without being entirely aware of the enriching dimension of it all. As grown-ups, we came to realize that the Alley had been the crossroad where young destinies had met and interfaced with each other for a short period of time: the moment of an encounter albeit brief, but existentially how significant!

12

MAMAN, THE BAKER!

Every Wednesday and Sunday afternoon, as soon as the shop closed, Maman baked cheese sticks, *Napolitains* cakes and fruitcakes. With it being half-day closing, the *commis* (shop assistants) were away and we treasured those private times with our parents.

Maman's pastry was separate from the making of our Potato Crispies (chips) that our parents made with a team of employees during the week. For the crispies, Papa had plastic sachets made in bulk. These were sealed with a machine once they were filled with crispies. Papa inscribed the bags manually with a sort of stamp with this inscription: «*Potato Crispies, Handy, Tasty & Crispy. Best for all occasions. Prepared and Packed by...*». With three flowers drawn by him on top of the label. Il seems that our Crispies were the first ones commercially made on the island! Our customers loved them, and we also distributed them to other shops as well as the Royal Navy in the neighbouring town. According to rumours heard by our brother J., it seems that Queen Elizabeth, during one of her visits to our little island, got to taste our homemade Crispies when she lunched at the Royal Navy!

We, children whose ages ranged between two and eleven in the mid 1950's, helped our parents in any way we could. On baking days, we stayed by our mother's side. We watched her with fascination. She was not even 30 years old at the time, too young to be a mother to six children. Our admiration for her skills increased with each passing year. As we grew up, we became aware that she had exceptional baking skills for someone without any formal training.

For the fruitcake, our mother gave us a pail in which we beat the butter and sugar. With our young hands, using a flat wooden spoon, we had to beat the mixture until it became all creamy. We, the older children, all took turns with this arduous task and handed the mixture over to our mom when she declared the batter creamy enough for the next stage. She would then gradually add the eggs and the sifted flour. When she was satisfied with the spoon test, she would pour two thirds of the batter in the baking tray, introduce the *glacé* cherries and raisins which she would carefully arrange in a circle all around the batter, then pour the rest of the batter on the top before putting the cake to bake in the oven. The cake would be ready after an hour or so, and the aroma of fruit and butter coming out of the oven was heavenly. We watched from a distance when Maman did the toothpick test. She would push the toothpick all the way down the middle of the cake to check if the cake was thoroughly cooked. She would bake a few fruitcakes during each session.

While the fruitcake was baking, our mother prepared the pastry for the cheese sticks. Her cheese sticks were popular with our customers, and were well known throughout the county; people from all parts ordered them.

The preparation of the pastry demanded precision: make a well in the centre of the flour and pour a little tepid water and some colouring in it; mix while incorporating with one's fingers big pats of butter into this "dry" dough until one gets a granular consistency; add lots of grated Tête de Maure or Gruyère cheese and knead gently until a firm pastry is formed. Finally, roll the pastry out until it is about one centimetre thick, making sure not to work the pastry too much.

Maman was very meticulous about getting the right kind of dough. Once she made sure the pastry was firm and not overworked, she would roll it out with her dusted rolling pin – which had been a long bottle for many years. Our mother worked at a large table set against the wall of the shop, in the open shed that was our dining-room. She used a marble slab to work the pastry. One corner of the marble slab was broken and we think that Papa must have bought it at a sale, or even second-hand.

I remember that we all learned how to cut the cheese sticks to help our mom. She taught us how to slice the pastry into strips that were around nine centimetres long and one and a quarter centimetres wide. The secret was to use a very sharp knife and do the cutting with a quick precise cut. In our case, we used a Chinese cleaver for the job. We acquired speed and precision with each passing year. The aroma of butter and cheese that pervaded the working area made one want to eat the baked sticks as soon as they came out of the oven. These cheese sticks were crisp and melted in the mouth, making them famous throughout the island. From time to time, we were allowed to eat one that got broken accidentally. We could not hope for many of these since any broken bit meant less profit for all the efforts and arduous work performed by Maman.

The *Napolitains* (Mauritian biscuits topped with icing) were made of two small shortbread circles (about one centimetre thick) stuck with jam and coated with a light pink icing. Our mother used to bake the shortbread circles the night before. She would do that after she had finished working in the shop and had cleared all the chores. She then worked well into the night. We sometimes helped cut the circles using an upside-down glass. We loved sticking the baked and cooled circles together using strawberry or raspberry jam, turning them into shortbread sandwiches to be iced the following day.

The icing was the most delicate part of the whole process. It was made with melted icing sugar to which a pink colouring was added. The moment of truth came with the icing process: it had to be just right. If too thin, the icing would simply slide off the circles, too thick and it would give a hard coating that would be lacking in sheen. The end result had to be silky in appearance and easy to eat. The shade of pink had to be an attractive pale pink that would please the eye and tempt the palate. When our mom prepared the icing, we were not allowed to talk, as she was tense until she got it right. Once the icing was ready, she had to dip the top of the shortbread sandwiches into the icing, give a sharp twist and place them on a cooling tray. When all the cakes had been coated, everyone was relieved. Only mom was allowed to take the tray of baked *Napolitains* to the shop and place them in the display cabinet for sale. We would at times be left with a few broken shortbread bits that we loved eating. We also looked forward to enjoying the bits of pink icing left on the tray. We would sometimes share them with our friends.

Now, after so many decades, I can still see Maman doing all this baking week after week, her back becoming a little more hunched over the years. I can still see her, with her hair piled on top of her head, face red with all the exertion of the preparations and the heat of the oven. I see her in her nylon or cotton overall worn for hygiene, and as a protection from all the flour, surrounded by us children, so happy to be able to help her and be with her. I can recall that at each whiff of heat coming from the oven, we experienced the warmth of family life all around us. And all this brought on such comfort to our young hearts!

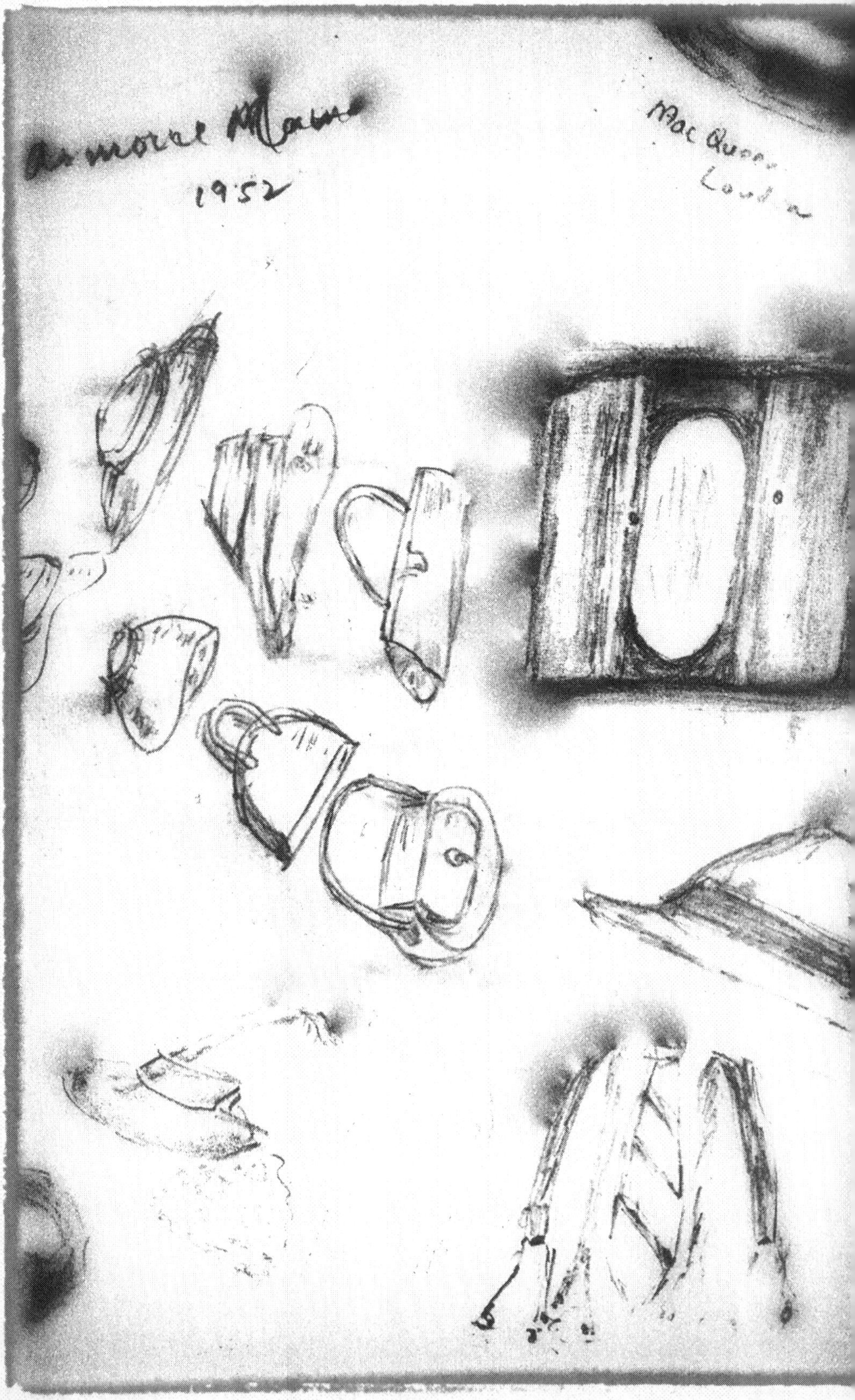
1952

13

MAMAN'S WARDROBE

Throughout our entire childhood, at least from the time we arrived in Quatre-Bornes around the year 1950, Maman's wardrobe was deemed to be an "institution".

This "Art Deco" style teak wardrobe was part of my parents' set of wedding furniture. It had three doors. The doors on both sides were curved, and the middle one was flat, lined with a large, tall mirror used by the whole family to inspect themselves before important outings. In the 50's and 60's, this wardrobe symbolized, for us children, a place where many treasures were kept; treasures that we were able to admire, touch, and hold in our hands only on special occasions.

These occurrences were very rare in our younger years. Our visits happened after requests made to our mother in the evenings when she had finished her work in the shop, and her other chores. They sometimes occurred when it was half-day closing at the business, especially on a Sunday evening when our mother had finished making the *napolitain* cakes or cheese sticks to sell during the week. Therefore these wardrobe visits were very precious: Maman always had something more important to do!

During those moments, we sat on small stools or on our parents' bed, waiting for her to open the wardrobe. First, we had to fetch the bunch of keys, a task assigned to one of us; then mother would open the two side-doors. These sections only contained a couple of grey or black suits of Papa's, or smart dresses of Maman's made of silk, or guipure - two or three outfits that they would only wear to important receptions (weddings or banquets). We did not spend too much time looking at those. We admired from a distance the tweed or fine wool from England or the superior quality cotton from Ireland of which Papa's suits and shirts were made. As well, we looked at the two or three pure silk ties hanging on the door. We were allowed to have a feel of the silky material of mom's dresses. We liked the fragrance of the mothballs or camphor protecting these clothes in the side compartments. Those smart outfits were without any doubt gifts from Papa's sisters who lived in South Africa.

Our mother then closed those two side doors to at last open the compartment we had been longing to see: the middle one with the mirrored door. Sitting in the "sleep" area of the large room known as the "salon" (the living room), we held our breath while she pulled on the door. The middle door was the most reluctant to open! It finally opened with the familiar creaking sound. Each time the suspense was worthwhile, as we knew what treasures laid behind it. Once the door was opened, our interest was stirred by the unknown, and the thought that since our last visit there would be new things that we had not yet seen. In fact it was, above all, a need to satisfy our visual, olfactory and other senses. It was also the nostalgic need to see again the ancient objects we liked. The whole expectation was cause for cheer.

The four shelves were roomy and could contain thousands of small treasures. On the uppermost shelf were the pretty hats belonging to our mother: the "cloche" hat or fur hat, the bonnet or the turban of the 1950's. There was the cream hat with a veil slightly on the side, the black polka dot hat that we called "the doll's hat" and which was worn tilted towards the forehead. And I remember a very large black hat with feathers of the same colour that our mother placed just above her chignon. Long pins used to secure the hats in position were kept on the side. Our favourite was the green velvet hat that was our joy as Maman allowed us girls to try it on. The first minutes of the visits belonged to the girls.

Matching the hats were small handbags and *cabats*, square or round clutch bags made of crocodile-type patent leather, or of Morocco leather of the same colour as the hats. We were in full admiration of the Spanish style mantillas, golden, silvery or black that covered our faces completely when we tried them on. When our mom wore them, she truly became the most striking woman in the world; beautiful, light of complexion, with dark hair and dark eyes! She could hardly have been more than 26 years old at the time.

What we loved to touch and fold delicately were the handkerchiefs that Maman kept in her wardrobe for us to use only for outings, such were their finesse and beauty. As little girls we liked those with colourful prints, of princes and princesses from fairy tales, of bees and birds, or of butterflies. When we became older, we admired the mauve or yellow wild flowers beautifully displayed in the centre of the fine fabric; or pretty girls surrounded by sprigs of flowers and leaves, with such words as: *"He loves me... Il m'aime... Er Liebt Mich ..."* As well, we loved the red big roses adorning the fine chiffon hankies.

We were also fascinated by the bottles of perfume, white or indigo blue, that mother's sisters-in-law gave her every year: Bourgeois, Cherami (or is it Cher Ami?), White Fire, Espace, and so on. The boys were more interested in trying on Papa's shoes that they took from the boxes on the last shelf; but they also had fun trying on Maman's costume jewellery: heavy necklaces and matching earrings.

After a few lively minutes, we calmed ourselves for the most sacred part of the visit. In the middle drawer, were those jewels of Maman's that had been her dowry, and that we were not allowed to touch. We could only admire from afar such items as a gold chain, rings and other gems nestling in velvety jewellery boxes. The necklace we admired the most was made of Chinese gold, bright yellow and warm looking, made of small discs shaped like small lacy hearts held together by fine links. One of the treasures was a Chinese bracelet made of exquisitely designed flowers, that could be adjusted to size by pressing on the flexible ends.

Besides Maman's precious jewels, Papa too had in this compartment his treasures stashed in a big Cadbury box. These were comprised of a variety of publicity objects from many companies: knives of all forms, shapes and colours, bottle-openers, oyster-openers and so forth. Papa also had in his treasure trove a couple of watches, sunglasses and one or two Parker fountain pens collected over two decades.

My sister S. and I became daring over the years. During our adolescence we "borrowed" certain items from Maman: scarves, belts, necklaces of imitation pearls that we wore secretly at Beau-Bassin, at Coocoo's when we went to parties. Afterwards, we put them back discreetly without our mom noticing. But sometimes, we simply asked her to lend us these items.

Alongside our memories of Maman's wardrobe, are those that we have of certain chests or sideboards that were placed almost by the side of the wardrobe or behind it. There were the green wooden sideboard, the yellow one and the brown one. These contained our clothes or various sheets or tablecloths, and even our shoes. They were made of ordinary wooden planks, but were nicely painted. These were simple pieces of furniture, but they were dear to us who did not own much, since they brought us the kind of comfort that only objects constantly present in one's daily life can engender.

However, we cannot refer to Maman's wardrobe without talking about the space "behind" the wardrobe. "Behind-the-wardrobe" is a spot that has remained firmly anchored in the collective memory of our family. This famous innermost recess was associated with a number of activities. Situated diagonally, the wardrobe separated the "sleeping" corner from the "living room" area, as it were. So "behind-the-wardrobe" was an ideal recess for all manner of things. It was a place where we gladly hid when we played hide-and-seek; or we hid there, as children, to avoid adult visitors we did not want to meet; we played there quietly without being discovered. We went "behind-the-wardrobe" to get dressed once we became adolescents, as it was the only private place in our tiny maisonette, where one could undress, away from the eyes of others. As the corner was blocked off and protected by a curtain, we girls felt very secure to dress there everyday. There was a chest there, where our mom kept special things about which we knew very little. We espied, from a distance, silk articles: traditional ancient men's costumes that our grandfathers might have worn in China around the year 1910; women's slippers; Chinese dresses probably worn by our grandmothers when they left their motherland in the years 1920 - 1930.

Therefore, as well as being a place of practical use, our mother's wardrobe - and the space "behind" it - was a small repository for the past, its treasures and its memories.

Visits into Maman's wardrobe became more rare with time, especially for the boys who had other interests at fifteen. For sentimental reasons we girls visited the wardrobe when we returned to our island on holidays. With our mother, we would look at those shelves with great nostalgia. After Maman passed away, and then Papa, we browsed through the wardrobe for a last time all together, to see what was left. We each took one or two keepsakes to pass on to the next generation. Through these objects from our past, we wanted to share with our children those simple, innocent but precious moments of our childhood.

14

T'ONG HA AND YOUNG BHOR

I had two *Ah-Bhors* (grandmothers). One of them was Young Bhor, my mother's mom. While Ng Bhor, my dad's mother, represented comfort and safety, Young Bhor symbolized gentleness and peace. She was a shadow haloed with kindness, who always watched over us.

During the 1950's Young Bhor had become an ascetic. She lived like a saint who had virtually left this world. She was *Vegan* and she ate very little. She lived in the pagoda called "Tong-Ha" which was on Pope Hennessy Road in the capital city: a two-storey building, which housed altars dedicated to Buddhist deities. I recall that, as children, we were always slightly frightened of the Hindu god adopted by the Buddhists: Hanuman, the "Monkey god". The various services of the temple took place in the main part of the building and, at the back across from the courtyard, were the living accommodations.

Young Bhor occupied a small room in the rear of the compound, and lived there for a while, having become a lay devotee of this small Buddhist community. When we visited her, our grandmother used to prepare some special dishes for my sister S. and me. She thought that we would not be used to her vegan food. At times, she bought us fish balls from the snack bar across the street (called "Meeting Chinese"). With these, she would make a delicious soup that we would pour on our steamy rice. However, most of the time, I wanted to taste any vegan food she ate, for in my view it was tastier than the food we were fed with at our shop in Quatre-Bornes.

She had the use of a small corner of the big communal kitchen to prepare her meals. When the food was cooked, we sometimes took it to her small room for our little supper, but we often ate in the sheltered area of the rear veranda where a few tables were set. This served as a dining room for the congregation, including the girls who were aspiring to be nuns or abbesses: Ah Sui Tsao, Ah Lee Ti, and others. Oftentimes, we played together in the rear courtyard after supper; besides the *Sap si Waye* (the feather and ankle game), there was the game involving the use of all our fingers and tiny sand bags (*sai pao*): endless but fascinating. We played on the cobbled floor of the courtyard, in the midst of all manner of activities being performed by the adults.

Around 1956 - 1957 during our visits, we lived a carefree pre-adolescent life (my sister S. and I were around 10 - 11 years old at the time). Young Bhor and the other nuns let us purchase ice-lollies or other goodies (such as pickled mangoes) from the small snack-bar across the street, and on rare occasions, they even allowed us to go to the cinema at the Pathé Palace, a few steps from the pagoda, to see "non-X" films, that is those suitable for children. Etched in my memory is the fragrance of the flowers of the Oleander bushes in the front garden, along the wall that lined the street. It impregnated our late afternoon outings with a sweet, pungent and somewhat romantic air. This scent awakened our senses, as we were soon to grow into young adolescents.

After these outings, we had to rush back as the girls of the congregation had to join the priestesses and nuns for their evening prayers. We felt that although these young friends shared some of our childhood pursuits, they were not like us. Even at our age at the time, we knew that a different destiny awaited them. We therefore looked upon them with a sense of puzzlement, and even a certain respect. These teenagers were novices who took their role seriously even if they were occasionally allowed the freedom of acting like other young girls. In the evenings, we used to join the prayers of the religious community and the devotees like Young Bhor, who lived a religious lifestyle quite remote from the secular world. They were an inspiration to us young girls.

The session was long, though we took pleasure in praying with the Buddhist chaplet, the *mala* (*Niam Fu Tsu*), a rosary of 108 beads perfumed with sandalwood – we found this scent quite exotic! While the officiating priestesses and adepts were reciting their *mantras* with the *mala*, we would use the beads like a Catholic chaplet without understanding much of the prayers. We tried our best to kneel on the cushions the Buddhist way, as well as to join our fingers in a kind of "fist" with the thumb inside the other fingers to imitate the devotees. On the whole, we did recollect ourselves; we did meditate in our own way.

We loved the somewhat spicy aroma of incense, the chanting of the priestesses and nuns, and the sense of peace that prevailed. However, this peace was sometimes shattered. S. told us about the day when, during a special ceremony, a crystal vase on one of the altars exploded loudly after a long session of chanting: it had been a sign from the deities; the answer to a request from the priestesses, of a tangible proof of their divine presence amid this assembly of the faithful!

The congregation at T'ong Ha was comprised of nuns and novices, and in line with the Mahayana Buddhist tradition (The Big Vehicle: *Tsin Zin Fut T'ong*), it also involved a lay community. A few of these women were not simple "nuns". We later realized that these were more like abbesses (*Tsu Mu*) – two or three of them - who administered the affairs of the pagoda, led the ceremonies, rituals and prayers. These few were rather like women-monks, who were qualified to officiate at various ceremonies. I am referring to them as "priestesses" and not as ordinary "nuns" for it would not be surprising that these Abbesses had acquired in Taiwan or Hong Kong – the original places of their training – the same rights as the women-monks called "Bhikunis" - the *Sanskrit* term for "those who renounce…". Unlike other regions where Buddhist nuns were traditionally subordinate to men monks, in China historically (and later in Hong Kong and Taiwan), the nuns' organizational structures were, during many centuries, separate at all times from those of the men monks, thus affording these women formidable powers in their sphere. Therefore in China and some other countries where the Mahayana Buddhism is practised, women monks or nuns can receive the full "women monk" ordination, equal in rights to those received by "men monks". These terms are used here in the general sense of "priestesses" and "priests". (Bhikkuni Dhammananda, 1999)

Growing up, we learned that in Hong Kong and other countries, there were priestesses or women-monks with exceptional knowledge. These obviously followed in the steps of an endless line of predecessors. After all, in the sacred books like the Pali (one of the earliest Buddhist Canons), there are multiple references of many outstanding *Bhiksunis*, from the very beginning of Buddhist history. It is told that the most learned of these religious women had succeeded, during their many years of training, in committing to memory the *Tripitaka* (the *Sanzang* in Chinese) - the Three-fold Knowledge of Buddhism - that is, the whole sacred scripture of Buddhism!

Somewhat like their sisters from the past, the abbesses we knew were imposing in their personality. Their presence was that of simplicity and sobriety, yet of great distinction.

At T'ong Ha, the next generation would thus be trained by female religious leaders whose expectations of the young novices were high: the abbesses trained them not only in the monastic aspect of Buddhism (the scriptures, principles, rituals, and so forth), but also in the administrative and regulatory facets of running a temple and its congregation. The girls we knew were anywhere from 11 to 16 years of age. We saw them try to memorize Chinese Buddhist scriptures and chant them loud. Their religious life involved not only the daily prayers or services, but also special feasts and ceremonies, which spread over the whole day or several days. Big dinners were given to the devotees and visitors. Vegetarian dishes were in order at the banquets organized during these feast days. Many dishes of meat were replaced with "imitations": that is, these meats were made with only vegetables and beans. For example, *Foung Moun* (red pork) looked exactly like the real thing, but was made with Tofu and its products. The whole vegetarian banquet, proffering splendid "meat" platters, always looked amazing to us children! Hence, the novices had to be taught all the intricacies of religion, as well as those of running the pagoda, including the organization of big "meat" banquets.

After prayers and meditation, at night before going to sleep, Young Bhor would talk to us. It was mostly one sided, since we answered her as we could due to our very basic knowledge of Hakka. It could well have been during one of these quiet conversations that she told us about having met in the village of Kung Kung (our grandfather, her betrothed from the age of five), his grandmother who wore a veil covering part of her face. As a young child, she had been intrigued by someone who did not look like the rest of the family and who dressed differently. She learned later that the veil indicated that the grandmother was a Muslim, and she had come from "a faraway country..."

At the pagoda we spent mundane moments intermingled with spiritual ones; that is to say, Tong-Ha allowed us to develop social pursuits of urban life (cinema, visits to street vendors and so on), but also gave us the opportunity for new experiences where deities and spirits were within our reach, and even within our "touch".

After our stay with Young Bhor at the pagoda, it was with a rather heavy heart that we returned home. We were happy to see Papa, Maman and the boys soon, but also a bit sad to leave Young Bhor and this place we knew to be special, even at our young age. We left T'ong Ha with nostalgia, for there it seemed that we had tasted for a short time, in a small way, multiple facets of a puzzling, mysterious and fascinating world.

15

PAPA'S "TREASURE CHEST"

On rare but very precious occasions, Papa produced his large Cadbury chocolate biscuit and toffee tin from the wardrobe. This box was a large one that must have contained innumerable cookies and toffees. One of his friends had given it to him, all emptied of its contents. Some other children had savoured all these toffees while in LaBoutique (our shop), we were only occasionally allowed the toffees sold at retail from the glass containers. When this happened, we appreciated not only the beautiful taste of the toffees, but also their golden or silver wrappings that we carefully flattened with our nails to make "pictures" to keep preciously in our notebooks or books.

It was only on some special occasions that Papa opened his toffee box, or rather his "treasure chest", to show us something precious he had acquired, or to give us one of these objects to mark our academic achievements. It was his way of showing his pride in us for either having won the "petite bourse", the primary scholarship that allowed us free secondary schooling at private schools, or later, for having passed with honours the Cambridge Senior Exams or the Cambridge Higher School Certificate. When we were to begin our further studies either in Mauritius or in Europe, his proffering of one of his treasures was to wish us luck for the new life, our first tentative step towards adulthood.

Our survey of the box, or rather of its contents, was very quick because he never opened the box widely enough for us to have a good view, but half-opened it just long enough to take out the special gift that he had chosen for us to mark the occasion.

The teak wardrobe was known to us children to be Maman's possession, whereas the toffee box that was kept in there was Papa's. From the various "visits" into Maman's wardrobe, when we had a brief peep into our dad's big box, we knew that the box contained two top quality Swiss watches. These he had collected over the past two decades. To augment this small collection, over the years our dad bought less pricey watches from his brothers who were importers of such items. He sometimes displayed these watches with pride (pride for our success as much as for the quality of the object) as he offered one to each of us, in turn, when we won the greatly coveted primary scholarship. I remember that the one my sister received was silvery, with a dainty face, the wristband made of beautifully fashioned interlinked circles. Mine, when my time came, was somewhat bigger, in chrome, modern with square elasticized links. For the boys, the watches were the classic types for men.

Also preciously kept in the box were two pairs of sunglasses, bought with savings from the past several years, again of top quality and of a renowned brand (one was a Ray-ban). Papa probably kept them to offer to the boys later on.

In this chest, he also kept oyster openers – sturdy little gadgets made of metal with a pointed end – which he produced during the oyster season. For a while it was a red one (a St. Raphaël). The "ritual" of the oysters took place in the evening, after the shop had closed. During these special occasions, we children sat around him and the box of oysters to observe how he opened them with one of the tools taken from his treasure box.

In our younger years, we did not know exactly what Papa's box contained. But if we became cognizant of its content during our later years, we must assuredly have transgressed some rules! Did we not, one day during our teenage years, break the rules when our parents had left us alone with the maid? Did we not stealthily creep into our parents' bedroom and open the wardrobe using the key that was kept in the chest of drawers?

Indeed, whatever ruse we had recourse to, one fine day, we were able to open wide the "forbidden chest" for a thorough examination of all the contents! There, we found a variety of pens, including one Parker and one Sheaffer, and his favourite, an Eberhart. A few of the items in the box were expensive, but most were publicity items, or items that cost very little, but were of great interest to us. We could never have imagined the extent of Papa's collection. It would have been fairer to refer to it all as his "collections". There was a range of pencils advertising Mauritian companies such as: The Mauritius Cold Storage Co. Ltd. (*New Moka St., Port-Louis*); Louis Barbés Pougnet, *Commission Representation* (*10, Bourbon St., Port-Louis*). Foreign businesses had their fair share of publicity too, such a: Milk Stout Simonds – Hop

Leaf. ("*Made in England*": was it the milk or was it the pencil that was "*Made in England*"); or Mercury butter, *affordable and tasty*! (Again, "Made in England": pencil or butter?); and finally, Amstel *Holland Beer*!

Also, we saw Papa's collection of pen nibs, which we were told were at times melted to produce rings. It seems that Maman's wedding ring had been a product of this kind of enterprise! In addition, there were his tortoise shell bits, which he later chiselled into delicate rings for us girls.

That day we also discovered the penknife collection: small, medium and large. They were advertisements for Martini or Black Label, brands that Papa liked? Or did he collect them simply for their variety of colours, forms and sizes? We found large multi-bladed red ones, a minute single-bladed blue one, and a very large dark red one with lots of blades, a corkscrew and a nail cutter.

And what about the key holders? They varied in shapes and were made of different materials. The gold Cointreau cube shaped like a bottle, the flat square in gold and red for Prior ("*Please return these keys to Prior Marseilles...*"!); L'Elf Antargaz (*Marine Road Quay D, Port-Louis 2-5930 08 – 8047/8*).

We admired the series of blotting paper of different companies. We also found a small brooch with the picture of Jacques Désiré Laval (1808-1864) embossed on dark metal. The jewel in the crown was Papa's old fob watch (probably dating from before the 40's), attached to a chrome chain by a leather ring, which he very rarely wore.

There were other "collections" – not in the box itself – but in its vicinity on Maman's shelf: bigger items that could not fit. Namely, red or blue and white jugs advertising spirits such as Red Label or White Horse Whisky. There were also a number of glasses advertising Black Label or Johnny Walker.

In the years that followed our "rummage", every time Papa partly opened his box of treasures, we could not look him in the face. We kept our eyes downcast through guilt. The happiness at receiving the object was somewhat tainted. For after the day of the great discovery, we felt that we had left childhood behind. We had, it seemed, definitely moved on to adolescence and beyond, where subterfuge and cunning merge with the white purity of innocence to create a state of consciousness both grey and confused, the kind that leads to adulthood.

16

Papa's Treats

When we moved to LaBoutique (our shop) in Quatre-Bornes around 1950, we felt quite deprived. Even though we were surrounded in the shop by a multitude of candies and delicacies, these were out of bounds to us, the family. They were to be sold for a profit for the financial survival of the business. We had to pay a hefty amount for the lease of the building; we also had to provide for our numerous employees and ourselves what nowadays one would call "healthy nutrition", that is, some rice, lots of greens and a bit of meat.

However, though we felt deprived compared to the children who often came to buy sweets in our shop, we were to get some sort of compensation amid what we children considered as "deprivation". This came in the form of various treats from Papa.

After attending early mass on Sundays, our father would bring us hot *pootoos* that he bought on the porch of LaBoutique Rosaire, from a merchant there. These were fluffy white Indian cakes full of grated coconut. The rice cakes were steamed and came out extremely hot from the long narrow cylindrical moulds in which the merchants steamed the *pootoos*. We liked eating these fuming hot with our morning tea. They were moist yet not soggy. Sugary yet not sickening. They were light and fluffy, yet filling and comforting. How special these cakes were! What treats for a Sunday morning!

Also, every Sunday, Papa would invariably make us Sardine sandwiches. These were special, not so much in terms of their content, but because of the process he followed in making them.

After his Sunday mass and the opening of the shop, as soon as he would have a minute to spare from the morning business, Papa came to the courtyard to make the treat.

Each time, Papa proceeded in exactly the same way. He took a thick pat of *Plumes* butter from Maman's large butter can in the pantry, put it on the table in a container, and let it soften there in the mild sun. A bit later, he came back to beat it and soften it even more with a large fork or spatula. The butter was then mixed with some English mustard, salt, pepper. As soon as the mixture was blended and smooth enough, he added what in his view were the best sardines in the world: those soaked in olive oil, from Portugal. Using a fork, he slightly crushed the fish in the pungent paste. He finally split some crunchy pains-maison where he spread his preparation generously enough without being too copious. We relished in these crispy treats for brunch. We, his children, were in awe of his ability to produce such a delicacy. That he, who was unable to fry an egg for himself when needed, and was always served by Maman like a king, was indeed capable of such culinary surprises. What a marvel, we thought!

The other kind of treat that is intimately linked to Papa in my childhood memories is that of our occasional oyster feast. Even now, each time I eat oysters, I inevitably think of my father.

Every now and then, when it was the season, we would receive for sale to our customers, a huge batch of oysters from our suppliers, fresh and sea smelling. By the time we reached the age of 10 or so, we were already aware that Papa loved these molluscs. As we knew that he could not resist having some during the oyster season, we naturally expected him to treat us to these. We looked forward to these evenings when Papa would put aside several oysters at the back of the shop for us to enjoy.

Papa went through a complete ritual for the opening and eating of these delicacies. Before anything else, he soaked them for several hours or overnight. Then, as an essential preliminary to the opening process, there was the brushing of the shells, which was to get rid of the sand and dirt.

Our feast usually took place either on the stone steps leading from the inner courtyard to LaBoutique or, if the steps were wet after a downpour, in the merchandise room (*samm marsandises*). We enjoyed sitting on the cold stone steps in the fresh air. But if we had to savour the oysters indoors, we were also content sitting on the "balles" (sacs) of rice or legumes in the storage room, with all sorts of oil or petrol metal containers around us, and at our feet small bags or mini-crates of oysters that were to be sold.

I remember that we all sat expectantly around, and waited for our dad to bring his soaked and cleaned delicacies. We felt a certain excitement since we knew even at our young age that these oysters were expensive (having been imported from Rodrigues or Madagascar, I can't recall which). We knew that it was a luxury: our father was at fault for spending so much money on us; but we were happy to be his accomplices!

For a start, Papa would go and get his oyster-knife. This was usually a publicity object from French aperitif wines, such as St.-Raphael or Dubonnet. These short rounded knives were specially made for oysters and were very effective for the safe opening of the molluscs.

The opening itself required caution, since one could easily get hurt if the knife slipped from one's fingers. So the best way was for Papa to use a cotton towel to protect his fingers. He would open the oyster tentatively at first, by inching his tool towards the small opening in the shell, then by thrusting the knife slowly into the crack. A little "crack" sound meant that the knife had penetrated the rough shell opening, and had created a slit big enough for the knife to slide in and be slightly twisted inside the oyster to open it widely. With a small brush, Papa then cleaned any debris from the appetizing flesh. All he had to do before we actually gulped it up avidly was to squeeze some lime on the oyster to acidify the fishy taste. The sheer succulence of it: we loved it all!

It was all simple enough and yet took a great significance in our minds either as young children, or young adults. It was a big step into adolescence and adulthood in so far as these oyster feasts introduced us to the fine world of gourmets. All that we lacked to complete the gourmet meal was a bottle of Laurent Perrier.

Papa clearly showed his skills in the matter of oyster opening, but most importantly, he succeeded into transforming the simple opening of oysters into heart-warming reminiscences, which we have preciously kept from those times of our childhood in LaBoutique. By offering his treats (his oysters, his sardine sandwiches, his *pootoos*), he showed us a side of him that was intimate and non-threatening. At those special feasts, we forgot that it was this same Papa who could threaten to give us a good beating with *rotin-bazaar* (beating cane) after some serious misconduct. Now that our father is gone, I think of this harsh and serious facet of him, but what remain most of all are those moments of implicit understanding, even some sort of complicity, between him and us, when we became his equals for a few hours; when he briefly took the time to be one of us, creating moments of sheer warmth and closeness which we, his children, will treasure forever.

17

RAILWAY STATION IN
QUATRE-BORNES

Every weekday at about 7.30 a.m., dangling our small satchels and *tentes* (soft rustic local baskets), my sister S. and I made our way to the railway station to catch the 8.00 a.m. train to school. Our Catholic school, "Notre-Dame des Victories", was in Rose-Hill, the next town along the railway line. Our parents chose to send us there as opposed to the local government school as the school was reputed for "bagging" the highest number of Junior scholarships in the region.

We started taking the train to school when we moved to the shop in Quatre-Bornes around the years 1951 - 1952. Each morning, I followed my sister closely as I was still very young at the time. I was only six and she was seven. She was bigger and stronger than me and charged towards the station at full speed.

In the early 1950's, the train was the most popular mode of transportation on the island. It was a steam locomotive. A huge amount of coal was needed to produce enough steam to power the train up unusually steep inclines, a distinctive feature of our island's landscape.

At the time, we were puzzled enough by the train and the way it worked. And little did we know as children how interesting the history of the train system of our island was. It was much later that we learned all about it. During the second half of the 19th century, the fast growing economic and industrial sectors of the island called for the development of a modern and efficient mode of transportation for passengers as well as freight (mainly for the sugarcane industry). As a result, Mauritius established one of the best railway systems in the British Empire. Being modelled on the British Railway System, it was very efficient too. At its peak, the Mauritius Government Railways boasted 52 steam engines, 200 passenger carriages and 750 freight wagons. (Jessop, Arthur, 1964:8)

However, things changed when lorries were introduced around 1920. Over a few decades these became the transportation of choice for freight. Consequently, this competition caused the railway service to steadily lose money. After many years of financial loss, The Mauritius Government Railways had to be made redundant. The passenger service ended in 1956 and the freight service in 1964. I remember the last passenger service of our great railway system. It was in September 1956 during the visit of Princess Margaret.

Quatre-Bornes was on the railway line that linked our capital city of Port-Louis to the most important towns (Mahebourg - Rose belle - Curepipe - Rose Hill). This line was the second to be built in 1865, only a year after the first one. The railway station was a small white timber-clad building with a grey roof. It was plain enough to look at but had that " British Colonial Establishment" air about it. In short, it was the typical railway station of a British colony: clean and imposing.

To get to the station, we had to walk along Route Royale (later named St. Jean Road). The short walk was accompanied by the jolting sound of the wheels of ox-driven carts and by the engine noise of occasional cars. Reaching the station, we experienced totally different sounds. A "toot toot" and the loud noise of grinding metal announced the arrival of the train. We were soon shrouded in soot, coal dust and smoke that penetrated our lungs. It was interesting to watch the stoker work and feed coal into the firebox. Once on the move, the metallic noise changed into the hissing and rather soothing sound of the steam engine. Later, when we emerged from the train, we did not mind having particles of soot on our school clothes or even smelling of smoke.

Whenever we arrived early at the train station, after buying the tickets (if Papa had not already bought them), we made our way to the platform to wait for the train. The few spare minutes allowed us to observe the adults who were going to work; most of them going to Port Louis. They must have been Civil Servants and businessmen, the former dressed in smart khaki suits (colonial in style) and the latter in light-weight linen suits. In those days, women rarely went to work. The few ladies on the platform wore cotton dresses, knee length as dictated by the fashion of the day. They were fairly young and may have been nurses or teachers. There were a few senior pupils from the Loreto Convent Schools, Queen Elizabeth College or other Colleges. We could tell by their uniforms. There were no children of our age; either their parents drove them to school or they attended the local school.

It was in fact at the station that we saw, almost everyday, S. and D. We might have been young children then, but we did notice some interesting details. They were known to be sweethearts and they always travelled by the 8.00 a.m. train. It was amusing for us children to observe them holding hands in public. They must have been only 16 - 17 years old the first couple of years we saw them on the platform. Sometimes we dared go over to say "hello" as they were our uncles' friends; and at other times we just waved and smiled. They were a striking couple; D. a dark and handsome young man, S. a beautiful dark-haired girl. To our young minds, they were the best-looking couple in town!

With all the confusion on the platform, my sister sometimes lost our tickets. This meant that we had to board the train at the very last minute because we had lost time looking for our tickets. At times we found them in a gag on the platform. Whenever we could not find them, we had to go to the stationmaster to explain (we did not want to pay another few cents for each ticket). Luckily, he knew that Papa was in the habit of buying the tickets in advance. He was very kind to settle it all for us, and allowed us on the train.

The return journey was usually quite boring. At that hour in the early afternoon, there were no adults coming back from work. We alighted at Quatre-Bornes and made our way home sensibly, without stopping by the shop near the station. The owners were family friends. We would go directly home without daring to dawdle in front of Pelma with its displays of luxury goods from Europe: embroidered linen table cloths (from Alsace); fine Guipures (from Paris); and worn by blond-haired dummies, lacy blouses (from Ireland). At the crossroad at Bernardin de St. Pierre Street, we would glance briefly at the windows of Vues Modernes. We would satisfy our curiosity by having a quick glimpse at the display. My sister, precociously aware at her young age of the celebrities of the day, could name for me the various personalities pictured in the window case.

There were Photoplay magazines featuring famous actors such as Paul Newman or Elizabeth Taylor on their covers; Paris-Match with photos of Prince Rainier of Monaco, Princesses Margaret and Elizabeth of England (who would become Queen in 1953); or the Shah of Persia. Besides these photos, we also admired other interesting items such as pure lambs wool capes and jumpers (Sayelles), De Lux soaps (Yardley), and beautiful dolls with large blue or green eyes and long eyelashes.

This was our daily journey to and from school. Once home we quickly changed into the old clothes we wore in the house, that is, our *linzes-lacaze*. The nice clothes were strictly kept for schools and for outings. After an early dinner, we did our homework. When we were old enough, we also helped our parents in the shop, normally at the till, for from a very young age, we had to learn calculate the change to give to our customers (no cash register then!).

During the quieter moments in the evening, we used to reminisce about what had happened at the station in the morning, thinking of the characters we admired and aspired to emulate. We also tried to recall all the shop windows we had passed on our return journey. At night our young dreams would be of all those adult figures and luxury goods, of the various moments at the station - all blurred by the vapour of the engine and the hissing sound of the steam. The tooting of the train would lull us gently to a soothing and rewarding sleep.

18

THE HAUNTED HOUSE

It was a winter afternoon in 1954. I must have been eight years old. After school, I had edged my way to the other side of the road. It was probably around 4:00 p.m. My brothers and sister were changing into their *linze-Lacase* ("home" clothes) and I, having changed very quickly, had decided to go on a little walk without the others.

I was wearing my short pale yellow coat, somewhat faded due to the constant wear from me, and before that from my big sister S. who had worn it during the previous winters. It was a checked coat, quilted in the Chinese way by Maman or Ah Bhor (my grandmother). It was like a sailor suit, double-breasted with two rows of white buttons.

As usual at the time, fixed onto the left-hand side of my coat, I had a safety pin that held about ten clinking religious medals. These were of various figures: the Virgin Mary, our Lady holding the Infant Jesus, St. Christopher, St. Joseph, St. Anne, St. Anthony, St. Bernadette kneeling in front of the Apparition, and other saints.

One wonders why a small girl of my age wore, attached to the front of her clothes, for all to see, such a big bunch of medals that clinked with every step she took! I must have had some good reasons to do so. It was after my First Communion, so that I must have already been warned about spirits (angels, devils) that ruled this world and beyond. There were also the often-repeated stories the maids told us about the forces of good and evil of that other universe that did not have a place within the Catechism we were taught. Was it to protect myself from the evil spirits in that other world, or from the *loups-garous* (werewolves) or the *nâmes* (ghosts) that populated these tales? Without any doubt, there must have been a multitude of complex reasons that explained my dependence on those medals.

It is true that the island has always had an iconic culture. There was most certainly a cult for saints and their replicas prevailing at the time - more evident then than nowadays. Most Catholic families on the island owned an oratory that allowed them to pray to the saints of the Catholic faith, and my medals represented more or less the same statues standing on our home oratory. Even nowadays, people on the island like to venerate saintly statues through religious processions, when they walk across towns or villages with great devotion, behind a life size statue of the Virgin (on "Our Lady Day") or the Blessed Sacrament (on the Feast of the Blessed Sacrament). There is also the tradition of visiting shrines of holy statues (For example, at "Notre-Dame du Grand-Pouvoir", people pray to the Virgin Mary).

So there is no doubt whatsoever that my obsession with medals partly derived from our culture, a culture of statues and other "replicas" such as religious medals, all of which were generally believed to have protective powers. The astonishing thing is that no one influenced me in that direction. If I wore all these medals, it was not at the request of my parents or some other adult but simply because I felt that I needed protection. It was the instinct of a child who wanted to ward off some evil presence! It was indeed thanks to my clinking medals that I acquired locally the mocking nickname of "Bonne-Femme Médailles" (little lady with the medals).

That afternoon, sporting my hand-sewn coat and my medals, I strolled along the main road (Royal Road, in the 1950's), and crossed over. At the time, it was quite common to see children crossing the road on their own, without their parents, for Quatre-Bornes in the early 1950's was still like a village. Road traffic was almost non-existent in the afternoon; buses and cars rarely passed through. There were occasionally ox-driven carts that school children liked to follow with the hope that the carter would give them a piece of sugar cane to chew on to enjoy the sugary juice.

So, crossing the road at leisure, I made my way towards the small wooden house. A glazed veranda, much like all the other colonial houses of the period, fronted it. My parents rented that house for our uncles and the *commis* (shop assistants) who could not be accommodated behind the shop. The bamboo hedge surrounding the property protected it from view. The house was set in the middle of a garden that looked quite abandoned, as the tenants who changed from year to year did not take care of it. In front of the veranda, the parched lawn was dotted with a few wild roses that looked like old ladies who had survived against all odds; still, they cheered the place up. Borage and dying shrubs more or less concealed the outdoor toilet situated at the bottom of the yard.

That day, the dusty and parched garden looked even more desolate in the timid winter sun. The entrance did not have a gate; it was partially blocked by a peach tree whose fruit was ever so often stolen by school children on their way home from school. Apart from the movement of the rare passer-by, it was in an atmosphere of almost complete stillness that I went through the front door of the house; it was never locked during the day. Wearing my Chinese cotton shoes, I tiptoed across the veranda towards one of the bedrooms but there was no one there.

I must have been looking for my uncles, Kiew Kiew or San Kiew, for certain. I often sought the company of my young uncles when Maman and Papa were busy in the shop. Suddenly, I heard a strange noise coming from one of the rooms. It frightened me, and I made my escape by padding very quickly towards the back door.

The day after my discreet mini-excursion on the other side of the road, I heard the rumour that must have started the day before: the house across the road from the shop, the rented house where the shop assistants lived, that house was haunted. A *commis*, who was in the house the day before, had noticed the sudden appearance of dusty footprints. These trailed from the entrance hall towards one of the bedrooms, and ended by the back door. It was a mystery, he thought, that those footprints should have appeared so mysteriously, for according to him nobody could have entered the house without him noticing. He had called out as he went to have a good look at the strange footprints but there was not a soul around. What an enigma! According to the other occupants of the house, nobody had announced any visit for that afternoon. After many enquiries with the people in the shop, it was ascertained that no one (no servant, no shop assistant, nor a member of my family) had been in that house on the afternoon in question. Anyway, my brothers, my sister and I were supposed to have been helping in the shop after school and after our homework. Papa was very strict and did not allow outings without special permission during term time. The holidays would not start until a week later.

Rumours ran rife for the next few days. From then on, nobody wanted to sleep at the small house. Everyone was afraid of further ghostly apparitions or manifestations of some evil entities. There was now the question of where to house everyone. It was a matter of having to convince them that the house was safe. Our parents would probably decide to send for the priest to bless the house. Amid all the discussion, the suggestion emerged that there might have been in the past some gruesome occurrences in the house (murder? suicide?); or was it a case of werewolf? Listening to my parents' suggestion, the *commis* suddenly remembered that yes, he had heard a strange sound just before he noticed the mysterious footprints. Yes, indeed, he had heard some sort of clinking noise. According to him, it was, without any doubt, the noise of... no, not the noise of a werewolf ... but ... On hearing what he was trying to recall, I paled, and by some sort of reflex, touched my bunch of medals. My young instinct told me that I had better make myself scarce. So, surreptitiously edging my way through the bales of rice in the storeroom, I went to hide in the tavern by the side of the shop for quite some time!

It must have been since that incident that I began to lose interest in my precious medals. I decided from then on that I would not wear them anymore - or, if I did, I would wear them inside my clothes. And I locked them in my drawer for many months for fear that the truth would come to light. To this day I have kept quiet on the subject: the fear of a child who had caused such a hullabaloo for the adults of our small community.

In our neighbourhood, the small house became known from then on as "the haunted house": the evil house where harmful apparitions took place, even in the afternoons, in broad daylight.

Several years after this incident, the "haunted house" was demolished. People said: "Good riddance": the *nâmes* would fly to better pastures! As for me who had felt this little tinge of guilt all these years, without the sight of the house across the street, I finally felt guilt-free about my little "mischievous" footprints!

19

AT TANTE NETTE'S

It was in 1957. Every Sunday afternoon, at around 4.00 o'clock, the bus would reach the terminal in Port-Louis, our capital city. There at this final stop buses from all over the island ended their journey. From there, I would begin my walk to Tante Nette's house. Being such a young child to have to live in another town away from my parents, I had left LaBoutique (our family business) with a certain sadness. We lived in Quatre-Bornes but I had to spend my weekdays in Port-Louis at our aunt's to go to school there.

Tante Nette's house was at the corner of Madame and Enniskillen Streets. Rue Madame was a strange street, large and very straight, with a set of canals running parallel to it on one side. The canals were part of the drainage system from the time of the French rule almost three centuries ago. I always felt that this was an endless road. For my young limbs, these canals seemed to run along a very long distance. They started from Les Casernes and the hospital. Les Casernes was a French colonial compound built by Labourdonnais before the mid-18ᵗʰ century. There, a branch of the British Army had its headquarters during the British rule.

It was only after a good half hour (that's what it felt to me) that I reached the end of this lengthy and impressive system of canals: the last one ending in the neighbourhood of Tante Nette's front porch, on Rue Madame, not very far from the foot of the Montagne des Signaux.

It was a typical middle-class house, small and quaint, in the capital city of Port-Louis. It was painted white with a grey roof, charcoal trimmings and white shutters. It was probably a remnant of many French colonial-style houses and buildings erected over several decades in Port-Louis in the 18ᵗʰ century, at the time of Labourdonnais and Cossigny. From that time resulted, amongst other major constructions, an assortment of small and big wooden houses with grey tiles, some of which were built at the very edge of the street, without any front garden, but "right on the road" so to speak. Tante Nette's house followed that latter model that is still to be found in some small towns in France.

The courtyard at the back was the space for private family time but at the front the windows opened directly on the streets. The only screen from public view or street noise consisted of curtains or shutters which protected us from the intense tropical sun as well. When we opened the shutters or blinds, leaning slightly to the right, we could admire the whole panoramic view of Montagne des Signaux. As a child with a vivid imagination, I sometimes thought I could perceive in the crystal-clear sky of Port-Louis, on the far side of the mountain, the life-size statue of Marie Reine de la Paix (Our Lady of Peace). The stately figure held a beautiful and mysterious aura of peace and majesty around it. Sometimes at dusk, here and there on the side of the mountain, there were small fires burning in mild flares and igniting that side of the city with soft red and orange embers.

The dusty streets in Tante Nette's neighbourhood were quiet. They were almost free of cars. Port-Louis at the time had a relatively small number of cars - compared to nowadays. It was the fifties, and the cars we saw were large British cars with all sorts of wings and trimmings made of chrome. More often than not, the modes of transportation were bikes and public buses. Shorter distances were covered on foot. Carts or carriages ridden by an ox, a mule or a horse were not an uncommon sight. Carts driven by mules were frequently seen transporting on the streets of the town loads of merchandise for the various wholesalers of the capital. The smaller retail shops had only hand-drawn carts to carry products (monthly "rations" of rice, lentils, flour) to their customers. The island then was very different from what it has become now at the beginning of the 21st century: it is obvious that Mauritius in the 1950's had not yet started the era of modern transportation for private individuals.

The only people who were known to own a car at the time were the C. family: they ran a huge black Chevrolet (which to us looked like an old Rolls Royce). We would always look with admiration and a certain envy at Mrs C. when she drove that car with great celerity some rainy mornings to drop off her many children at school. Sometimes, we would see her place her young son in a taxi-cart from the mews located at the side of Tante Nette's house. The cart, hired by a teacher, would be shared with the boy to go to their school located at the other side of the city.

There at the stables, we could hear workers repairing the cart wheels and maintaining the forge by blowing into it. I seem to recall that in winter - which is rather mild in Port-Louis - street children who were sparsely dressed in rags would keep warm and have fun helping to blow the fire.

At the back of Tante Nette's bungalow, beyond the courtyard, was a renovated compound called "dépendance" (built for some ancillary use in former days). This consisted of a couple of comfortable rooms. In one of these, our grandmother Ah Bhor lived. Beside her room was the dining area where, on afternoons and Saturdays, Tante Nette gave private tuition to a great number of students, including me. Further at the other end of the compound were the kitchen, bathroom and lavatory.

The courtyard was a place where all the chores pertaining to the preparation of meals were performed. These included the winnowing and cleaning of grains and legumes like lentils in big *vannes* (flat baskets), the shredding of vegetables, the crushing of spices on the *roche-cari* (curry stone), the drying of carrots and cauliflowers for *achard* (Indian pickled vegetables). There, Ah-Bhor used to dry her Chinese mustard greens to make *Kon Ham Choy*. In addition, in this space she also did her crochet and knitting, producing nice vests or jackets for us. She also made, in that same spot, cotton slippers and shoes for use even when going out, or wooden clogs called *K'iak*, used mainly by adults for baths or showers. In fact, all manner of tasks were achieved in that open, sunny courtyard; it was a pivotal area where daily essential activities were performed.

For some of these activities, Ah Bhor was often helped by her cousins who frequently visited her. My grandmother was the most westernized of them. She wore a dress at an early stage, as opposed to the *Sam Foo* (Chinese top and pants) which the cousins wore most of the time.

But what I remember the most is the room Ah-Bhor occupied with Say Coo. A room where it was always good to spend time. Being there was a bit like going back home. Besides Say Coo's warm presence added to Ah Bhor's, this was due mostly to the various scents that came from the room and reminded me of the ones I had grown up with at our shop. These nice aromas came from balms our grandmother utilized to massage us, her grandchildren. We always sought the comfort of Ah Bhor's massages to cure all our ailments. She used Mentholatum or Tiger Balm, or other homemade concoctions made of herbs, alcohol and roots (like *Tah Yok Tiu*). She knew which vital spots to massage to heal our pains. Later during her adolescence, our cousin D. would have her fair share of Ah Bhor's massages after her ballet lessons each week.

In that small room, Ah Bhor and her cousins had long chatty "pyjama parties". They talked far into the middle of the night, about their past in China and their natal village, and also about the world of spirits and ghosts. Ah T'ai was the cousin with the funny eye, who could see spirits (those of the dead), and "felt" them near the door at night.

During my stay with them, Tante Nette and Seesouk (my uncle) were the kindest of hosts. Even though they had a very heavy load, having already one toddler and a new baby, they indeed did their best to welcome me. And it was a full house. Was our youngest uncle there at some point? Was he at the time working and saving money for his Engineering studies in the United Kingdom? Whatever the case may be, I certainly remember him as this tall and slim young man, studious and serious, who took care of us in our childhood, giving us constant support and helping all through our lives (even giving us Math tuition later during our Secondary School years).

As *zenfants* LaBoutique (shopkeepers' children), we were introduced to new horizons thanks to Tante Nette. She always gave generously of her time doing lots of charity work, including annual *Fancy Fairs* (fundraisers) in Port-Louis. The Chinese Community Fancy Fair was a grand annual event that we attended with her. It lasted from morning to dusk and involved a multitude of games, lotteries, fun rides: in short, enough things to make a child or adolescent go crazy!

Another big event of the year where she took us was the Maiden horse race at the Champ de Mars in the capital city. She used to walk with us amid the crowd, and buy us treats local to our little island: *gato-piments*, *badjas*, *samoussas*. Spending the day at the Champ de Mars in the warm sun of Port-Louis, watching the races, munching on all these goodies, and drinking lemonade, was a dream-like affair for us who came from the "country-side".

Our aunt could cook a wide variety of dishes, albeit with the assistance of her maid. She was instrumental in introducing us to foreign gourmet dishes. It seems to me that it was she who taught us, her nieces, how to make French dishes like Béchamel au Poisson, Gratin à la Morue, and Sauce Blanche aux Chou-choux. I can recall being exposed for the first time to "European" aromas in Tante Nette's house: *Daubes* (French stews) perfumed with fresh thyme, toasted bread fragrant with melted butter and marmalade or jam, and other "non-Chinese" dishes! These were things we were not used to as children of LaBoutique.

Indeed, Tante Nette was in my view as a young child a multi-talented person. She produced embroidered tablecloths, doilies, and handkerchiefs to be sold at Fancy-Fairs; she managed all sorts of crafts and was well-versed in almost anything worth knowing for a woman. With the help of her seamstress, she sometimes made us beautiful things to wear - generally once a year. She taught us embroidery and needlework (specially the "Smock"). From her, we learned how to behave like "young ladies", how to delicately and subtly use certain discrete perfumes – just a touch on the neck or on the wrist...

She would be considered a "super-woman" in this day and age: attractive, with a pair of greyish eyes and striking complexion, sociable, bright and generous! In her spare time, she helped others in the family or in society. Surprising how she found some time for others, besides her load as a mother, a full-time teacher, and her private tuition after school. However, of all her talents, her most remarkable one was that of teaching. Tante Nette's "lessons" were well-known amid the members of the Chinese community on our island. She was a teacher at the Loreto Convent in Port-Louis for many years and during her long career taught a wide range of subjects there, including Math, Geography, Languages, Home Economics and Religion.

In the afternoons, her teaching-room was crowded with youngsters of around 10 or 11 years of age, all of them seeking extra help after school. The ultimate goal was to win the primary scholarship that would guarantee free secondary schooling in one of the best colleges of the island (*Royal College, Loreto,* or *Queen*).

In my case in 1957, it was decided that I would have to leave my family in Quatre-Bornes during weekdays. I was to stay for one year in Port-Louis to attend the "elite" school called the Loreto Convent Primary School: that move was supposed to ensure a scholarship to study freely at any Loreto in any town, including Quatre-Bornes. That primary Loreto School was reputed for the high calibre of its students and that of its teachers.

During my stay in the capital city, I benefited fully from Tante Nette's private tuition. Her love of teaching was reflected in her devotion to her pupils. Be it in Mathematics (Arithmetic at the primary level), Languages (French Grammar by Claude Augé), Social Sciences (Geography of Mauritius by Ardill), her passion for teaching was felt in the way she would take a copybook and a pencil, and walk her student step-by-step through each question. It was something in her body language: her pleasant voice, her handling of the pen or pencil, and the mental process she went through stage by stage to explain the problem! Her passion and extraordinary gifts no doubt instilled the love of learning in her pupils.

All her former pupils have memories of her as one of "the best"! I have met many of them over the past decades: she is always very fondly remembered as "Miss Nette" - and who, in Port-Louis and elsewhere on the island, has not been taught some time or other by Miss Nette? Indeed, I am always very proud to say that she was my aunt.

Populated with interesting faces, jotted with new discoveries and enriched by unexplored places, that period in the capital city was to be of tremendous importance in my development: from being a young child I grew into becoming a preteen girl ready to face the challenging world of adolescence. Imbued with such experiences, my time at Tante Nette's will always bring me sweet remembrances!

20

LORETO CONVENTS

It was in the 1950s. My sister S. was already a pupil at the Loreto Convent School in Quatre-Bornes. She was the second Chinese girl to attend the school. In the years just after the war, the island was still regimented by a colonial society. The difference in social classes was a reflection of an economic reality. There was the segment of the population, established on their big estates or properties, who lived in luxury, and the others (including the recent immigrants and other communities) who did not have much. Only the affluent attended the Loreto Schools, the Royal Colleges, and the St. Esprit College.

But, over time, as of the 1960's, the situation gradually changed. The "others" began to save money to send their children to these private institutions. Some families, including ours, began to benefit from the government scholarships that would allow their children to be educated at those schools destined for the well-to-do.

The Loreto schools in Mauritius have a long history. In the early 19th century, there was no Catholic school on the island. It was in November 1845 that the first Loreto Convent opened in Port Louis as a Boarding School, with added to it a free day school for poor children of "all races" including those of Indian origin. The fees paid by the well-to-do students attending the Boarding School were used to subsidize the free day school. Later, an orphanage was added to the Loreto complex. This first Loreto educational institution, opened by only seven sisters sent from Dublin, was initially located in Bourbon Street but later in 1860 was moved to La Corderie Street. (Loreto Convents: "The First Loreto Community in Mauritius, http://www.ibvm.org)

In those days, frequent epidemics caused by the insalubrious climate of the coastal plains including the capital, Port-Louis, encouraged the nuns to open another Convent in the healthier highlands where the climate is cooler. As such in 1871, the Loreto Sisters Congregation opened the Convent in Curepipe. After changing locations several times, the Convent in that town finally settled in the town-centre near the church of Sainte Thérèse, on a lot offered by the Diocese. (Loreto Convents: "History of Loreto in Curepipe", http://vintagemauritius.org)

The Convent in Port-Louis was opened around two decades after Mother F. Teresa Ball founded the first one (named Loreto Abbey) in Dublin. She was one of the *Loreto Sisters* of the I.B.V.M. (*the Institute of the Blessed Virgin Mary*) - not to be confused with the Loretto sisters of the *Loretto Community* founded in 1812 in the United States. The I.B.V.M. was founded in 1609 by the visionary Mary Ward who championed the education of women even at the time. Hence the education of young girls is the main objective of any Loreto Convent in the world. Today, the Loreto Sisters run worldwide about 150 schools and educate at any given time around 70,000 girls. It is to be noted that the Loreto Convent of Port-Louis was among the very first in the world. In fact, it was founded earlier than that of Toronto, Canada (1847), that of Manchester in England (1851), and those of Australia (1875) and South Africa (1878). (www.ibvm.org)

My sister and I spent only one year at the primary level at the Loreto Convent of Port-Louis. We appreciated the warm welcome of family and new friends, as well as of teachers (Miss I.) and nuns (Mother A.) in our new environment. We had to spend a year away from home to attend that school that was reputed to "produce" numerous Scholarship recipients. I recall that I walked to school every day with my good friends F. and M. and that we spent a lot of time together even after school hours, either studying very hard, or chatting and playing games. After our brief time in Port-Louis, my sister and I began our Secondary years at the Loreto Convent of Quatre-Bornes, our town.

On the island in those days, most of the Loreto nuns were called "Mothers" – and oftentimes, they were referred to as the "Ladies of Loreto" (Dames de Lorette) - but in the 1960's after Vatican II, they all began to be called "Sisters". These nuns came mainly from Ireland, England or from the local upper class. As a result, the majority of the nuns were White. In the 1950's as young girls, we could not help but notice that those nuns who were not White but "Coloured" (usually of mixed ethnic backgrounds) were employed in the kitchen area or other parts of the house that pertained to domestic matters. We could see them in the cloistered part of the Convent when we looked for a nun out of school hours. More often than not, a dark skinned nun would answer the door. However, things changed gradually over the years when women of other ethnicities acquired an education and became the equals of the White nuns.

At first sight the nuns, wearing wimples and long black habits in the winter - and white ones in the summer - appeared to form a homogeneous group. But upon closer inspection, we were able to take their individuality into account. For example, there was Mother T., short and plump with a slow and poised bearing, sporting a "moustache" which looked newly grown but which was, no doubt, in existence for donkey's years. Then came Mother C. and Mother A. who were tall and noble and moved around with a haughty ease and grace. The nun, whom everyone remembers straight away without having to think, is our Mother E. who was slim, fair of complexion and prone to blushing. Always smiling, she called each one of her pupils "darling this", "darling that" with her strong Irish accent. We will always remember her as this radiant being full of life. There were also two White Mauritian nuns (Mother M. and Mother B.) who were sisters and came from a Quatre-Bornes family. They were pretty and gentle.

What was the rapport between the Loreto girls and the nuns? Being reserved by nature, I was shy in their sometimes intimidating presence; but generally speaking, the great kindness of these nuns was very comforting to us their young charges. I remember that when we had stomach cramps during a certain time of the month, the nuns made us lie down in a small cozy office that smelled of polishing wax. They gave us a dose of "eau de Carmes" (for a long time I believed it was "eau de calme", that is to calm and soothe the pain). The remedy worked and we subconsciously welcomed the stomach cramps every month, so we could get the sweet medicine that contained some menthol and quite possibly a small amount of alcohol: this satisfied "the delinquent" in us. It was also an opportunity to be pampered by the nuns in a wood-panelled room with teak and mahogany furniture (luxury which did not exist in the homes of some of us).

Every morning, I walked to the Convent with one or two friends. And my sister went to school with her friends. Dressed in our school uniform and carrying a satchel, we had to behave and look serious as we were representing the Loreto institution. We took about five minutes to walk from our shop, or longer if we chose to walk slowly. We would pass the "Galeries Payette" shop before turning left into Bernardin de St. Pierre Road. We sometimes had to endure the teasing from boys who were in that spot as if by accident. But the teasing took place mostly after school. In the morning, we used to rush round that corner, then walk past the gates of the B. family, our neighbours who lived behind our shop. After this came a series of gardens behind tall bamboo hedges. Finally we would reach the Chinese shop opposite the Convent and the Church. My sister and I never went into the shop as the others did to buy sweets. We felt that if we did that, it would be a betrayal towards our parents who sold the same sweets in our shop.

School opened at 9.00 a.m. We assembled in front of the veranda of our wooden colonial-style building. Each class stood in rows, led by our class prefect who checked the uniforms and straightened the row while ensuring complete silence, especially during the prayers and announcements. During our last year at the Quatre-Bornes Convent, one of us would be made Head Girl. This person would be in charge of the whole student population and would lead morning prayers.

Religious feasts were celebrated in the pretty chapel on the south side of the Convent building. The chapel was then filled to capacity. The young girls looked impressive in their pleated skirts in a blue check material, white socks, and navy blue berets. They filed into the chapel like a small regiment of the British Army.

I remember that on Confession days, we generally had to go to the neighbouring church. There, we lined up somewhat nervously to confess our venial and mortal sins to the priest. If our sins were not too serious, we would strive to mentally compile a list of venial sins we might have committed unknowingly (that was just in case we ran out of sins to confess!). Best friends would compare the penance dished out by the priest. Those in the queue of the more lenient priest would get an easy penance, just a "Hail Mary" whereas those who were unfortunate enough to have joined the queue of the other priest (the one who was old and cantankerous) would get a whole rosary to be said on their knees, or else… The nuns would issue strict orders forbidding queue swapping.

Every morning after assembly, the pupils made their way to their classrooms which were situated on both sides of the central corridor of the wooden building, where everything (floorboards, desks, chairs) was highly polished. Our school was considered to be very "high class". The main Hall, to the East of the building, covered a large area. We gathered there when it rained heavily or when we were doing a "retreat" (days of intense reflection). It was spacious enough to accommodate the whole community.

Based on Mary Ward's vision, a Loreto education was to promote the very best in girls so that they would "do great things" in life. Following the Loreto tradition, the range of subjects taught was very wide and varied. From the very first Convents in the middle of the 19th century, including the Convent in Port-Louis, all the original Loreto schools taught languages (including English, French, German, Italian) and a large variety of subjects: Arithmetic, History, Geography, Music (Harp, piano, guitar), Needlework and Art. The syllabus in Mauritius continued to cover classical subjects such as Languages (French, English, Latin), Geography, History and Mathematics. Miss A. taught us Geography and Art. Miss B. history. The two misses G. instructed Catechism, Mathematics, French or Latin to us. To this day, I have brief nightmares where I pitifully fail a Latin literature exam (Homer or Virgil) because out of panic I can't recall one single word of Latin! At the time, the nuns did not allow the "sciences" to be taught at the Quatre-Bornes convent (they probably thought that the Darwinian theories would unhinge their girls).

The diversity of subjects taught by any one teacher was quite impressive. We appreciated those courses that introduced us to fascinating books: in English Literature in Form I, " Little women" and later on, Shakespeare (*Julius Caesar, Macbeth* - and in the senior years - *Hamlet* and *King Lear*); in French Literature, the fine works of Molière (*Le Malade imaginaire*) and Racine (*Andromaque*). We studied the *New Testament* (the Gospels) in Form 5, which I found much more interesting than the Catechism classes of the previous years taught in French. The Gospels had to be learned in English since it was a formal subject within the *Senior Cambridge* syllabus, and we had to sit for the final exam in English. (The non-Catholic pupils who chose not to learn about Christianity went to another room during our religion classes). Domestic Science, Art and other subjects considered non-essential or non classical were taught in a small wing of the complex.

Once a week we went to the library attached to the great Hall where we read a collection of books. I still remember some of the books. In form 1, I recall reading an illustrated book of bees with mysterious and fascinating personalities. What a joy, at age 11, to enter this magical world and get engrossed in the lives of those bees and share their adventures: each of them had a specific role and each one a distinct personality. It was a wonderful escape from the dreary little space where I, as a shop-keeper's daughter, had to live in, squeezed so to speak between a group of employees and our large extended family!

Lunch break was around noon. It would see us making our way towards the back garden of the Convent which was right at the bottom of the property, away from the main entrance. The garden was a very spacious one, for its length seemed to us young girls to run almost three-quarters of a kilometre. We were in groups. Some played volleyball and others sat on the lawn chatting. The wide pleated skirt we wore was ideal to keep us "decent" when we spread ourselves about the lawn. Besides, the length of the skirt helped: hemmed below the knees, it would be considered long by today's standard.

Our lunch, brought in our small *tentes* (local soft baskets) just as in Primary School, consisted of a *pain-maison* with a little bit of margarine and some sugar, and some spread or cheese occasionally, and an orange drink.

I played volleyball when I had the chance but I was never very athletic. Our conversations and activities were no doubt those of the youth of the time, and were not as sophisticated as they would be today.

In our younger years, we probably chatted about our studies, teachers and books. Did we share our secrets? Did we say which boys we liked? And who were our best friends? We certainly had lots of friends... but in later years, we probably talked about films and actors. I know that by the end of the 1950's and the beginning of the 1960s, when we were that bit older, we often chatted about our favourite singers, the preferred topic being Elvis - and his songs (*Love me Tender*, popular as early as 1956), and his arch-rival, Cliff. On the island at the time, it was definitely a case of *"camp Elvis* versus *camp Cliff"*.

We saw the beginning of the technological age in Mauritius. Television was a new invention. In the 1960's, very few local families owned a television set. Most of us considered ourselves lucky to own singles or perhaps long playing records (LP's). We listened to the radio at home. One of the songs we listened to and sang alongside the rest of the country was *"Il y a le ciel, le soleil et la mer"*. We would also listen to Paul Anka (*Diana*, already popular by 1957). And Adamo (*Tombe la Neige* which came out in 1963).

Hence, our lunch conversations would naturally involve those songs. After lunch, the assembly was done quickly so that we could be back in the classroom as swiftly as possible. School ended at 3.30 p.m. Ballet lessons were available to those who could pay for them. They were held in the big Hall after school - or during lunch.

Besides the winter and summer holidays, the year was broken by a few pauses. One of these was the annual "retreat" usually held around Lent, to allow us to meditate and "repent our sins". The big Hall was filled with desks and chairs. We were silent for two or three days except during the sermons delivered by the priest or the nuns. These were there to guide our meditation and encourage us to "become better Catholics", and to grow spiritually. On the whole we enjoyed the retreats (no classwork for a start). And in general, we believe that they did benefit us in many ways.

The several years spent with the nuns did indeed shape us spiritually, mentally and psychologically. The nuns worked hard at trying to instil certain values in us. Despite the defects of the system - the sometimes extreme discipline of the school - the nuns were quite successful, I believe, in turning us into responsible adults.

We studied at Quatre-Bornes for five years, after which we had to move to the Loreto Convent at Curepipe or Port-Louis for the lower and upper sixth form. When we joined the Curepipe Convent, my sister and I felt quite grown up wearing the blazer at that school, since it was part of the Convent's chic uniform. It was much colder and rainier in that town. The school was twice as big as our previous school, and was built in cement and cut stones. (Alas, we missed the cozy wooden building of Quatre-Bornes). The cold and damp in the large and draughty classes made us shiver all through the winter. We endured it all as we felt that the hardship was character forming. We were becoming young adults and we wanted to prove ourselves.

In the morning before 8.00 o'clock, we waited for the bus at a stop, a short distance away from our grocery store on the opposite side of the road. We had to leave early because of the earlier start at Curepipe. It was at that bus stop that my sister and I met S. We had never met her formally, but in our childhood we used to see her holding hands with R. at the train station in Quatre-Bornes. They later married. We also made the acquaintance of Tante S. Both S. and Tante S. were older than us who were only around 16 - 17: they both worked for the Civil Service in Curepipe.

S. had two children at the time. And Tante S. was not yet engaged to our uncle S. They were just good friends. But a few years later, they started going out and got engaged. We were delighted, as we liked Tante S. very much.

My sister had already spent a couple of years at the Curepipe Convent before I started. So she left a couple of months after I began my years there. For me, it was a new life. At the same bus stop, I met some interesting young men, including R.C. who taught at a school in Curepipe. Besides the excitement of leaving my school for a new Convent which was reputed to be a "posh" school, there were other factors which contributed to enrich my experience: the bus journey; the novelty of meeting new people on the way; and the forging of new friendships.

For a girl like me from a small town, it was a new experience to meet so many girls of a different background: girls like D., the brightest pupil in our class and T. her cousin. They were White. Their fathers were judges and they lived in those enormous colonial houses in the outskirt of town. As seen in some photos, their libraries were wood-panelled (mahogany), and held a large stock of classical books. I could not help comparing these libraries to the three worm-eaten books Papa owned and cherished; he kept these behind the door of our tiny veranda behind our shop. True, the tiny collection - Alexandre Dumas and Victor Hugo

- was to increase in size over the years by the number of Prize books we children would win from school. But looking at these girls in Curepipe, I was full of admiration, and felt a little sad too. To me who came from a rather humble social background, these girls seemed to have had the advantage of being born into an intellectual, social and financial universe that was far superior to mine. I believed that it was unfair to expect us - shopkeepers' daughters - to be academic equals. Our worlds could not bear any comparison, as a matter of fact.

However, the two years spent in Curepipe were pleasant. I have photos somewhere of a picnic organized by one of the White well-to-do girls at her family's seaside bungalow (her *campement*). The entire class was invited. I remember the Coloured girls, and the girls of Chinese and Indian ancestry in the group. The atmosphere throughout the day was warm. There was no trace of racism, but only friendship. A good indication of what the world could become one day, with such girls as leaders!

The academic calibre of some of the nuns at Curepipe was impressive. These nuns, like Mother D., having graduated from Oxford or Cambridge Universities, taught us the theories of Teilhard de Chardin. There were also other good distinguished teachers like Mr L., Knight of the "Legion d'Honneur" (France).

During our many years as students at the various Loreto's, we made friends with other girls despite the difference in our social status. At rare times, we received these school friends in our bedroom-lounge behind our shop - in the part of the room that was curtained off from the bedroom area where my parents and youngest brother slept (the other little bedroom where already five of us slept could not fit the latter, especially when our grandmothers or cousins came to stay). To those visiting school friends, we served lemonade or Coca Cola and biscuits. But I remember that those visits always made me uncomfortable, as I was conscious of the poor standard of accommodation we lived in.

And we were also invited on rare occasions by our relatively new friends. I felt a mixture of joy and trepidation when my school friend G. invited me to play in her garden once. It was a generous gesture from the daughter of a wealthy family towards the Chinese girl who had no garden to play in. Their estate, located across the street from our shop, was magnificent and I felt fascinated by the whole property.

The century-old trees and the large-leafed ferns provided us with shade and well-being. I was suddenly transported under a heavenly canopy, wrapped in a rippling veil of green. It was such a magical experience - one that I have carried with me to this day.

Year after year, we move away from our youth, but there is always a certain essence of things which remains in our memories. For me, the spirit of friendship at the Loreto's in Port-Louis, Quatre-Bornes and Curepipe is part of that essence which has remained with us the students during a whole lifetime, and has moulded us into better human beings.

Our numerous years with the Loreto nuns gave us an education enriched with human, intellectual and spiritual values. Those nuns were familiar to us because they were part of our daily life. However, it was years later that we girls came to realize that they were after all strangers, having come from a faraway continent and from a background different from ours. But they did come to us to take charge of our lives with remarkable courage and intelligence. Those brave and independent women, some of whom had been feminists in their own way by their teaching and example, prepared us adequately for a world that would become more and more complex. They equipped us with enough moral steadfastness to face a life that was to be ever more difficult for each of us. Inspired by centuries of tradition from Mary Ward and her followers, they taught us how to always "do much", in caring for others and selves. They wanted us to become independent women in a changing and sophisticated world which would no doubt be full of challenges. But we as Loreto girls would prevail, for after all, the Loreto Crest does it not contain this motto, *Cruci dum Spiro fido*? Indeed, our faith (*Cruci*) and our hope (*Spiro*) would triumph!

21

BEAU-BASSIN

I have often wondered what fascinated us so much about Beau-Bassin. We, children of Quatre-Bornes, liked spending time with the family there. Why was it that, for my sister and myself, as well as a couple of our younger brothers, the ideal holidays were or had to be at our aunt Coocoo's house in Beau-Bassin?

Was it because of N. and C., our cousins to whom we were so close? Was it because of the special affection those cousins had for us, and their constant generosity? After all, their lives were far from being easy, with six children in the family? Was it that at Beau-Bassin we did not have to follow our parents' orders (mostly Papa's) and did not have to help in the family business in Quatre-Bornes? There must have been several reasons for our fondness of the town, including the fact that being in Beau-Bassin, we felt we had moved up a step: for a few weeks, we belonged to a fashion shop as opposed to a grocery store! Whatever the reasons, for us children, especially for my sister and myself, the mere mention of Beau-Bassin even today immediately unleashes a flood of sweet memories!

Indeed, we always think fondly of this town whose history goes a long way back. It is said that the name "Beau-Bassin" itself comes from the fact that the village was built south of a pond or big pool (a *bassin*) that was a part of the Estate owned by a certain M. Bouchet of the East India Company. The sugar factory in Beau-Bassin built in 1788 was closed in 1818, and the parcelling out of the property created a Housing Estate which attracted business people, professionals and merchants. The agglomeration of Beau-Bassin came into being in 1877. It became a formal village in 1890. Together with Rose-Hill, its neighbour, it was elevated to the status of "town" in 1896. Both would become municipal sister-towns in 1950, under the administration of a Town Council and a Mayor, based at the Plaza in Rose-Hill. (Beau Bassin-Rose Hill: "History", http://bbrh.org)

A few decades after its creation in the 19th century, Beau-Bassin was deemed important enough to be on the railway line that transported to the capital city of Port-Louis passengers from the most important towns of the island, including Quatre-Bornes and Rose-Hill. But after the closure of the passenger service in 1956, without the comings and goings, and the hubbub of the old railway station, Beau-Bassin became a much quieter place, even if the transportation of cargo by rail continued for a few more years.

We liked this town and its eventful past. However, for my sister and myself, more than anything, Beau-Bassin meant Coocoo's house - which in fact was more than just a house. It was a shop fronting Royal Road, located near the old railway station that later on was converted into the Post Office and the Police Station of the town.

Even in those days (1950-1960), Coocoo's haberdasher's shop carried very little stock. As the children were growing older and our aunt had more free time, she set herself up as a dressmaker and used the premises for her business. To improve her income, she spent most of the day sewing. The counter of the old shop having remained intact, she used it as a sewing table. This was where she kept her Singer sewing machine, a selection of spools of thread, a measuring tape, a pincushion, as well as lengths of material belonging to her clients. Some of the fabrics were waiting to be cut into dresses; others were cut and were waiting to be sewn. Those sewn and assembled pieces were kept in a tidy pile in a corner where she could get hold of them easily for her clients' fitting sessions. We were allowed to watch the fitting once the client had put the dress on. The person stood in front of a long mirror; Coocoo moved around the client, placing pins here and there to adjust the original shape of the dress to fit the client. She would also do some tacking if it was necessary. She was very skilled at it, as we never heard a client scream "aïe" from being pricked by a pin!

We too were clients of Coocoo's. She was the one who sewed our dresses for special occasions (Chinese New Year, or when we were asked to be bridesmaids) - normally only once a year. We were grateful to her for her hospitality and helped her in simple tasks she trained us to perform (tacking the pieces together or ironing the cut out material to make the sewing easier).

Our aunt and her family lived behind the shop. On the ground floor, there was a bedroom that overlooked the backyard, a small paved area, dark and damp through lack of sun. There was also a living room separated from the shop by a dark wide corridor where the ironing was done and where the fittings took place. In the small dining room a staircase led to the attic. At the end of the dining room, down a couple of steps, was the small kitchen that doubled up as a bathroom. We took our baths there in the evenings when all the cooking was done.

During our long visits to Beau-Bassin, my sister and I were well taken care of by our cousin N. After supper, the latter would fill the small oval tin bath with hot water for us to wash in. We came out of those mini-baths feeling refreshed and clean; then we went immediately to the attic where we slept. There were two or three large beds for the six children and us, not counting some other family members who visited at times. N. always placed us near her in the bed.

S. and I remember being terrified of the dark corners of the attic. On each side were big dark empty spaces. We wondered what could be behind the walls in those unused areas. The permanent semi-darkness and the fact that nobody ever ventured in those corners fed our already fertile imagination. We had nightmares just thinking about these black holes. If we happened to wake up during the night, we dreaded opening our eyes, for fear of seeing something! We imagined seeing ghosts coming out of those unexplored regions. It was usually after hearing of the death of an acquaintance that our fear reached its peak. What if the ghost of that person suddenly appeared to us? We believed that the attic was the ideal corner of the house for a ghost to hide in, especially in all those mysterious nooks and crannies...

Such was our fear that we would only go upstairs if accompanied by one of our cousins. But the cousins, especially C., would often tease us by mentioning "Bonhomme Sounga" (entity known in popular beliefs), and other spirits who, they said, were hiding in those spots and were waiting for night time to come and attack us. When we were told years later that Coocoo's shop had been demolished, our first thought was that, finally, the ghosts in the attic had evaporated into thin air forever.

In the mornings, we normally stayed with our aunt to watch her work and help her. We were also allowed to help our cousins with simple house chores. At noon we had a light meal which at times consisted of local delicacies such as *gato-piments, pain frire, dhal pourri*, that we bought from the next door vendor. Time passed very slowly during those weeks of total relaxation. We read comics or, when we had become teenagers, we would be allowed to read romance magazines that were there to be rented out to customers. We talked a lot about our favourite singers or actors. We listened to the radio too: songs of Elvis Presley, Matt Monro, Sylvie Vartan and Adamo. We argued often, as in our group there were "enemy camps": the Elvis fans and the Cliff Richard fans.

Sometimes in the afternoons N. would take us for walks. We went to the Roxy cinema to look at the billboards advertising the new films; for us in those days it was a luxury to go to the cinema. We would cross the streets without any danger, for in the 1950's, there were few cars on the road. However, I still found Beau-Bassin much busier than Quatre-Bornes which was only a big village at the time. There were also more buses in Beau-Bassin as the town was on the bus route linking various parts of the island. Those buses came from towns like Quatre-Bornes, Rose-Hill, Vacoas and Moka, ending their journey in Port-Louis. Some evenings, in the 1960's, we would catch a bus going to Rose-Hill and watch C. play basketball with his team.

At other times during the day, we went to Balfour Gardens to enjoy the cool air, the trees and plants, or simply the quiet atmosphere away from the town centre. The giant tortoises were also a great attraction to us. These had been imported from the Seychelles Islands, probably in the last quarter of the 19th century, after their species on the island got decimated by navigators roaming the Indian Ocean in the past centuries. These unique tortoises seemed like creatures of a pre-historic era: they could reach 120 centimetres in length and up to 150 years in age. This is why we, even as adolescents, liked to come and admire these astounding creatures with their huge black shells move around in the mud of their large basin.

It was in those days, when we were teenagers, that we became victims of an incident which we will not forget any time soon. It was during one of our excursions to Balfour Gardens with a few friends. The group must have been between 14 to 20 years of age.

R.C. had organized a hike down to the Falls in Balfour Garden. We strolled to the garden, as it was only about fifteen minutes' walk from Coocoo's house. We were so excited to have all our cousins and our friends with us that we made our way there at full speed. We had taken a nice picnic to enjoy close to the fresh water at the foot of the water-fall. Once at Balfour, we decided to leave all our shoes at the top of the ravine, in what we considered to be a safe spot. The descent was quick and pleasant and we soon reached the bottom. We ate our picnic seated on some large flat stones and there we basked and lazed in sunshine. The picturesque and peaceful backdrop was magical. After the picnic, and a swim for some, we took the climb back at leisure.

We pulled ourselves up in the best way we could. It was heavy going after the amount of food we had eaten. Once we reached the top, we went to find our shoes. We were puzzled: these did not seem to be where we had left them. We became more and more incredulous when, after looking in all directions, thinking we had the wrong spot, we still could not find them. We continued to search everywhere. After many unsuccessful attempts, we felt totally deflated and had to accept this extraordinary fact: all our shoes had vanished - all fifteen pairs! Imagine our embarrassment: to have to get back home barefoot! For those who were from Beau-Bassin, it was only a matter of a fifteen minutes' walk, barefoot, in full view of everybody – and that was bad enough. But what about those who had to get back on the bus to their respective towns?

After the initial panic, it was decided that the latter would borrow a variety of shoes from the friends in Beau-Bassin, as it was out of the question to go on the bus without shoes! In the short term it was a painful incident: shame and humiliation, and the physical discomfort of walking barefoot on burning coal tar. In the long term, the shortage of shoes for each individual was subsequently felt for many months; for most of us, especially the younger ones who did not work, only one pair of shoes was allowed per year, whether they be new or second hand. It was a painful but valuable lesson that stayed with us for the rest of our life: be careful where you leave your belongings, especially your shoes!

With such incidents, our time in Beau-Bassin was not monotonous.

Going back home from those holidays spent with Coocoo and her family, especially N. and C., we felt a mixture of gratitude towards them for the kindness they always showed us, and nostalgia at seeing the wonderful moments we had shared come to an end. However, we felt happy to see our parents and brothers again. Our pleasure was tinged with some guilt that we had not been home to help in the shop for such a long period of time: we had freed ourselves of our lives as shopkeepers' daughters for all those weeks.

All in all, we were glad to get back to our regular routine as young students: hard work, compliance with Papa's rules. Our life was a straightforward one where our studies took precedence over everything else. A simple life, where the only pastime allowed to us girls by Papa was to watch the world go by from the shop doorway, provided we made sure that our arms were well covered and decent: "absolutely no sleeveless or low-cut dresses"! We would observe neighbours coming back from walks; servants and maids coming to the shop to buy provisions for their employers; the occasional ox-driven cart full of sugar cane.... we were quite content to return to our peaceful life in our little town of Quatre-Bornes, but we kept the memory of our moments in Beau-Bassin in a special corner of our hearts.

22

Ng Bhor (Ah Bhor)

Whenever Ng Bhor (whom we her grandchildren called Ah Bhor) comes to my mind now, I see the figure of a strongly built woman, full of social grace, always smiling and loquacious. She was down-to-earth, capable, and skillful in many things.

The earliest memories go back to our home in Rue Boundary, Rose Hill, where she frequently visited with her cousins (Ah Zhi Bhor, Ah T'aï, and sometimes, Soon Coo Bhor). They would normally stay several days at a time. I recall their conversations in their *Fengshun* Hakka, with lots of "Zhi" sounds (as opposed to the "Yee" sounds of Maman's Hakka from Meixian).

That was in the late 1940's and early 1950's. What did they do during these visits? Did they cook? Sew Chinese padded jackets or Chinese slippers for us? I recall that it was always quite an event having them. Somehow for a few days, the house became animated with their presence, voices and activities.

After that period, my remembrance of Ah Bhor goes back to a time when I was about 11. It was around 1957. She was then living with Tante Nette and my godfather in the capital town of Port-Louis. She lodged in a room there in the renovated "*dépendance*" (a low annex which had been of ancillary use in the past centuries). That unit was at the back of the main house, separated from it by a cobble-stoned courtyard. In that little complex there were several rooms including the kitchen, the bathroom and toilets.

That year, I had to leave home for the weekdays during a whole year to stay at Tante Nette's cozy and welcoming home to study and compete for the Junior Scholarship called *La Bourse Primaire*. Ah Bhor played an important role in my young life during that year.

I did not like to bother Tante Nette with my idle chatter since she was always so busy. Therefore, some evenings, I liked to go to Ah Bhor's room to spend time with her.

The other person there at the time was Say Coo, who lived with our grandmother in that small room till her marriage to Tonton A. I remember her showing me much kindness whenever I was there: I always thought she was so very pretty too, with her beautiful "godé" skirts of the 50's and her thin waist. Tonton A. was frequently there during the evening hours. Oftentimes, since he drove a car, they would go out.

I still remember Ah Bhor's room. It was overly cluttered with the big double bed for its two occupants, and the wardrobe and all sorts of things around it, on shelves or on the floor near the walls. Ah Bhor used to collect pieces of fabric, of all shades and shapes, which she would cut into squares and keep for the time when she would have enough for a quilted bed cover. She sewed these squares up either with a machine or by hand, and gave these beautifully patched and multi-coloured quilts to all her children whenever needed.

She was the one who in her small room in Port-Louis taught me how to crochet. It must have been at that time that I began to take an interest in making things, but actually the learning took place over the years when I was in High School, whenever I visited her later on in life.

One thing that helped create the warm atmosphere in her room was the smell of Mentholatum. Was it this particular scent that gave us comfort and made us feel secure in her presence? Was it because we knew she could heal all sorts of ailments, and utilized all sorts of salves to heal? Indeed, Ah Bhor used a large assortment of oils and *cataplasms* (poultices) in her treatment of various ills. Born with such talents, she was adept in massaging us whenever we felt a bit sick. She seemed to have a certain cognizance of what we nowadays know as "vital points". She would massage us from head to toe, rubbing the sides of our eyes, our throat, our neck and shoulders, as well as our joints. These massaging sessions were the most effective means of getting rid of various ailments, including headaches or insidious colds. I recall the role Ah Bhor's massaging and other treatments played in the recovery of her son NgSouk, after his stroke around the age of 50.

Ah Bhor was known in various neighbourhoods around her own village near Rose-Hill/Ste-Anne for her healing abilities. She used to go and visit sick relatives and other people, apply her homemade poultices on abscesses and infections, or massage those who were in pain.

My grandmother was also endowed with an exceptional oral talent. She possessed a social grace and eloquence that were outstanding in a woman with no formal education. May be that talent was "inborn", we always thought as we grew up. However, it could also have derived from the fact that, as a very young girl, she sat on a daily basis outside the classroom of her father. The latter was a scholar and taught at the village school in China. Even then as a young girl she was a fighter. She had no right as a female to sit inside her father's classroom with the male pupils of the neighbourhood. So she rebelled just by sitting outside the door to listen to her father, and learn whatever she could from there. We cannot be sure how much she might have grasped at that early age, but judging by the kind of wisdom she possessed in adulthood, she certainly retained a fair bit of knowledge from Confucius and other thinkers.

One of Ah Bhor's special talents was her gift for storytelling. Not only was she a born leader with the social skill that made her a popular figure within the community, but she could totally engage her audience with her stories of the past. With her smile and pleasant voice, she could captivate our imagination with the anecdotes of her past in China, in the Fengliang village in Fengshun County, which was, as she told us, almost mono-Xiang, having mostly the Ng's and the P'ang's as Xiang's (family names). She oftentimes recounted to her children the frequent incursions of the "local" people (the *Punti*) of the neighbouring villages. The *Punti* constantly tried to take over the lands of the Fengliang community. Though the arable lands were limited in the region as in most Hakka inhabited regions, other natural resources were numerous. These included a river and thermal springs. During these civil skirmishes at the end of the 19th century and the beginning of the 20th century, which followed in the tradition of their age-long wars with the *Punti* people, the men of the village fought with anything at hand, mainly pointed poles. The women helped them by hurling baskets of stones on the invaders!

In later years, when we were big enough, Ah Bhor and the other elders told us, the younger generation, about the 20th century civil wars in China, from the year 1928 on, and the Japanese invasion of their motherland in the 1930's, when 10-20 millions of their compatriots died. What remained most in the collective memory of the Chinese people - especially the members of our grandmother's generation - were the tragic events surrounding the Japanese invasion of China, the bloodshed of Nanking and Shanghai. From the capture of these two towns, the figures of 300,000 civilians slaughtered, and 80,000 women raped, became a tragic leitmotiv for all future conversations in China and the diaspora for decades to come. All these atrocities from the Japanese, it seems, were reprisals against citizens and peasants who waged a courageous guerrilla war against the invaders. These tragedies will be lamented on forever. Ah Bhor had already left China when some of the 20th century wars happened, but the tragic events reached the people of the diaspora soon after through the survivors who had been able to flee the country. The whole community abroad was shocked by those tragedies that caused the migration of millions of Chinese. The 1930's in particular witnessed the emigration of thousands of our grandmother's compatriots from the south of China, to Mauritius and other lands. (Sino-Japanese Wars, www.https://britannica.com)

However painful these memories, Ah Bhor could cheer up and talk about happier days as well. She liked to talk about the *San goh*, the regional song of the hills traditional to the Hakka people; and the role of the Hakka women – who have always had their feet left "unbound" she said, as opposed to women of other cultural groups in China who had their feet bound - a custom which lasted for centuries. What she loved reminiscing about was the hot water springs in her native Fengliang, that were so very useful for everyday life, and which were hot enough to "cook fish", according to the tales she recounted! We heard that, like many other communities, the villagers in Fengliang had mixed with the indigenous people called the "*Sheh*". These lived in the South of China, adjacent to the *Fengshun* region.

We heard about the beginnings of the family in Mauritius in the first quarter of the last century: modest, even poor—since they had to live in a rudimentary thatched bungalow in the poorer suburbs of Rose-Hill, with ten children to raise, and the shop going bankrupt. Later on, there was the conversion of the family to Catholicism – by a missionary called Père V., after which Ah Bhor became an extremely devout Catholic. This conversion to Catholicism was to add a "European" dimension to the lifestyle of our family, so much so that our aunties and uncles on Papa's side were much more "westernized" (*Fan Sin*) in their daily lives than Maman's side of the family. The evolution of father's family toward the West had an impact on future generations as well. Papa and his siblings inherited, from that time on, their "westernized" edge: the use of European languages and adoption of Western fashion earlier than many other Chinese immigrants. For, apart from their *Fengliang* Hakka, Creole became prevalent in their midst very early in the history of their integration to Mauritian society; they began to speak and write French (and English) from very early in their assimilation to the West. Even Ah Bhor came to speak the Creole language rather fluently. As well, the change occurred in the fashion Papa's sisters promptly adopted: short skirts, haircuts/perms, manicured hands, make up, and so on.

Ah Bhor had an immense influence on us, her grandchildren. Her personality, bright, energetic and welcoming, always brought comfort – physical, moral and emotional. There is no doubt that her presence in our lives at the different stages of our development into adulthood added multi-faceted riches to our youth. She transmitted to us all the knowledge of our history and our past. And with all the talents and gifts inherited from her, the younger generation has been well equipped to confront life's challenges.

23

YOUNG BHOR'S PASSING

Young Bhor was my mother's mom. Her death happened to be an advent of pivotal importance in my childhood. The week of her passing created a major upheaval in the family, since she was the first one so close to us all to pass away. It happened around the year 1958. And I believe she was a little older than 50.

I remember vividly the moment Maman was told her beloved mother had a very short time to live, and her heart-wrenching sobs in front of the pantry in the sheltered part of our courtyard that served as the dining room. She and Young Bhor had an extremely close relationship. Not only was Maman her eldest daughter, but she had also been there for her mother, in a role reversal, as a caregiver and "confidante", from the age of five. Maman always told us about how, in China, she and her brothers would wake up at dawn and go to the small kitchen in the courtyard. It was cold and dark and frightening, she used to say. They would light up the fire, so her mother did not have to go outside. My mother would also be the one to serve breakfast (a meal of *cangee* and pickles, and steaming jasmine tea) to Young Bhor and the family. Maman had always been protective about her mother, since the latter had been emotionally and physically frail all her life, and a single mother most of it.

Her relationship with our Kung Kung (grandfather) had been too complex to fathom. To us children, we were told that it was a question of concubines and lack of sensitivity on the part of the former.

Before Young Bhor fell into a semi-comatose state, she lay there for many hours. We were all around her to be of comfort to her. I remember the way she hatefully pushed away Kung Kung who had come to visit her in her final hour. All I can recall is that thrust of her arm while she was lying on her side, as if to literally shove him away with all the force she could muster in what would be the last moments of her life. The sheer presence of the one who had been the "antagonist" all her life had caused this surge of energy for a few seconds.

As children, we knew the history of their relationship: they had been forced to marry. Their respective families had betrothed them to each other since our grandmother was around five. And Young Bhor had been uprooted from her family to join Kung Kung's village from that tender age. Had she never loved him? Was there a certain kind of love a young girl could have nurtured for a fiancé from a very young age? Had he ever loved her in a certain way, as one loves a younger sister? These are questions that remain unanswered since no one ever dared ask them.

Young Bhor had become a devotee of the Buddhist faith late in life: she had even spent several years living at the pagoda (T'ong Ha) as a devout member of its lay community, until she became too ill to live there in her little room by herself. She had become an ascetic, a strict vegetarian (a *Vegan*). I can recall the small section of the big kitchen at the pagoda, where she prepared delicate little meals of tofu or tofu products and rice for herself, and for us, soup made with *van yan*s (fish balls) bought across the street.

She spent some time in Quatre-Bornes close to us before her passing, in her rented maisonette, at the back of a fashion shop. I remember her low chair in front of our veranda where she was always seated when she was well enough to visit us in our shop. She often said a gentle word in Chinese to us. Her habitual presence there was of quiet comfort to all.

She had been sick on and off for rather a long period of time. Her heart condition became worse, and she was given only a few months to live. Then came the week when we all knew that she was nearing the end.

Something occurred which I will recall all my life. Young Bhor had been in a coma for at least a day. However, she suddenly regained consciousness and became aware of our presence. The energy emanating from her, when she was supposed to still be in a coma, was eerie. We as children became quite frightened. To us, from the time she became comatose, she was no longer quite our Young Bhor. She was only partly the same person: her entity had already acquired a ghostly element. At that moment, all of a sudden, she began to talk, in a strange, raucous and panting voice. She told us that she had just seen a golden carriage, covered with vibrant flowers, which was waiting for her to carry her into a very bright place. The horses were white beasts of strength and beauty that would carry her forward to her heavenly destination. What a wonderful tableau she was depicting for us, her grandchildren.

Later in life, I read that in early Buddhism, monks used to follow Hindu customs and come to the home of the dying. They comforted the latter and the family by chanting verses beginning with these words:

"Even the gorgeous royal chariots wear out..."

("Ceremonies and Funerary Rites for the Dead", http://www.buddhanet.net)

I wonder now whether Young Bhor was referring to this "gorgeous royal" chariot when she last spoke to us! That strange flicker of lucidity was to be her last one, for it was the so-called final pre-death stage of sudden and unexpected wakefulness (*Tenfor Fooklin*).

Did they sit her up on that special stately seat before she passed? Or did they wait for her to breathe her last breath to promptly install her on that imposing chair? That day the Buddhist priestesses and devotees explained to the family that it would be an irrefutable proof that Young Bhor had attained the highest degree of sanctity if she was able to sit up on that stately chair even in death. Indeed, it seemed to me that she did sit upright there for a rather long while, dressed in a black Chinese-style robe and hat, while protective verses called "Paritas" were chanted around her. Pictures were taken to prove the advent of such a remarkable occurrence: for quite some time her photo in that crucial posture hung on a wall in the pagoda in Port Louis. Though the situation was completely different, her photo later reminded me of the sitting in the Lotus position of dying or deceased monks who to achieve self-mummification had put themselves through self-imposed fast and other means, a custom practised until the 1800s!

For us children, our first encounter with death, and especially that remarkable scene of our grandmother's seated position at her last breath, remains indelible. In spite of the sadness of it all, our experience was enriched with the awe we could not help but feel when faced with the figure sitting upright after the last breath had occurred, thus ending her life in that ultimate state of dignity.

The wake lasted a couple of days. The whole family and small community of mourners were assembled in the living room. The Buddhist rites of bereavement were performed by the priestesses and nuns of grandmother's congregation, and lasted hours on end. Later on, we learned that they were a celebration of her life as a woman - her specific qualities, her achievements – at every stage of human development from birth to death. The chanting of the religious community produced an endless mantra meant to comfort the bereaved, but as well, to help the deceased person's good energies to be released from her fading entity. Amid the burning incense, one could hear intermittent contemplative verses from the "Sanzang" or "Three Jewels" of the Buddha: "*I take Refuge in the Buddha, I take Refuge in the Dharma, I take Refuge in the Sangha...*".

There were also the endless hours of mourning: formal and informal. The bereaving was very expressive. There were quiet sobs from my mother and my uncles; one could also hear family members and friends chanting phrases of sorrow and "impromptu" verses of praise directly addressed to the departed. These were often interrupted by the rather loud wailing of a group of women who were, according to an oriental custom, set up to wail and chant at wakes. All happened in a low rumbling noise sporadically interrupted by the high-pitched wail of some woman, or the voice of someone intoning yet another set of chanted verses.

The funeral took place a couple of days after the passing itself. It was to be held after another short wake at the *Kwoneh* (the family Club). All I remember is that in the mild tropical sun (was it winter time?) we had to kneel, out of respect, at the entrance of the small front yard, and even on the street curb, to let the coffin pass. The women and girls, including my sister and myself, had donned white capes and white hoods, white being the traditional colour of mourning. We also had green or white rosettes made of fluffy wool adorning our hair. Men wore a black armband. Those were the Chinese and Buddhist symbols of mourning for the close family of the deceased. At the point of departure from the house, the funerary cortege was accompanied by firecrackers - as a celebration of a life well lived.

The images of our Young Bhor's departure from this life will remain forever in our memory. In a way, our experience of our grandmother's passing moved us to a stage in our lives when we began to understand the finality of things, as well as the suffering and loneliness of the human condition. But if Young Bhor to us as children had represented suffering in her destiny as a woman, we began to realize at the moment of her death that she had become bigger than a mere victim. She had triumphed beyond all suffering, transcending into a life of distinction and enlightenment. She had lived as a noble character, and departed in a dignified and stately fashion given only to a few to experience.

24

PROMENADES IN PORT-LOUIS IN THE 1950S-1960S

ATTRACTIONS OF THE CAPITAL CITY

We as youngsters growing up in the 50s - 60s liked to have trips to the capital city of Port-Louis. We enjoyed the old city, its colonial buildings and its twisted roads with their old paved looks reminiscent of the centuries of colonial occupation of the island. This past is still reflected nowadays by the residences built at the very edge of the street with a courtyard at the back. Even to this day, many bigger houses have a side porch that in the former days was utilized by carriages and horses to reach the courtyard of the property. Our capital city is an old town with still many traits of the colonial eras, of both French and English administrations.

Port-Louis is indeed steeped in history. During the Dutch occupation, around 1638, this town was already in use as a harbour. Named in honour of King Louis XV under the French rule, it became in 1735 the main port and the administrative centre of Ile-de-France (the island's name during the French occupation). Well protected from strong cyclonic winds by the Moka Mountain Range, it was selected to house not only the main harbour but also the fort on the island. The French governor at that time, Bertrand-François Mahé de Labourdonnais, contributed in a colossal way to the development of the city by building lofts, an arsenal, an arms factory and a hospital. Potable water was supplied to the citizens by the aqueduct that was built along the Grande-Rivière Nord-Ouest. The labour force performing all this construction consisted of African slaves and workers from Madras. ("Port-Louis, Mauritius ca. 1650 - ", http://www.blackpast.org)

After the French era, during the Napoleonic Wars (1800–15), the port greatly helped the British Administration to gain control of the Indian Ocean

Every corner of the city seemed to bear some historical significance. Thus, during our youth, we were deeply attracted to this old capital so imbued with history. And we went there often.

First of all, the trip from our small town of Quatre-Bornes toward the capital was in itself truly pleasurable. For even before reaching the town, we were afforded a magnificent scenic view of the port. This vision of our capital always left us moved, and proud of the beauty of our small island! Going downhill from Beau-Bassin, somewhere close to Coromandel, we would be struck by the panoramic sight of the old port appearing against a backdrop of azure sea. The liquefied silhouette of the port seemed to mingle with the honeyed haze of the sky and the rutilant mist of the ocean. The heavenly view would slowly emerge and materialize in the faraway sky, as if from another world.

After experiencing such splendour, we would slowly enter the outskirt of town, and reach the terminal. A short stroll would take us to the various places we liked to see before we visited family and friends.

We enjoyed a nice walk along the road leading to La Chaussée and towards the Jardin de la Compagnie where we liked to sit on one of the benches in the little city park. We enjoyed the cool air and the shade offered by the impressive banyan trees (*pieds-la-Fourche*) that grew there. We also liked to go to the Musée de Port-Louis where the main object of our interest was a reconstructed model of the Dodo. This species that was unable to fly and survive had become extinct by the end of the seventeenth century.

After a brief stroll along an avenue of striking flame trees sporting their fiery red canopies, we would reach L'hôtel du Gouvernement. This imposing historic edifice was built by Mahé de Labourdonnais. There the Superior Council of Ile-de-France sat during the decades of French Administration, followed by the English Administration when the island became British in 1810.

Having enjoyed the impressive view of the avenue and of the administrative centre of the capital, we liked to pass by the Théâtre de Port-Louis. The first British governor of Mauritius, Sir Robert Farquhar, inaugurated this theatre in 1822, about ten years after the British conquest. The Théâtre de Port Louis was one of the first theatres to be built in the Southern Hemisphere, and hosted theatrical and lyrical troupes throughout the 19th and 20th centuries. For a long winter season, Mauritian and international artists regularly performed at the theatre (Port-Louis, "The Municipal Theatre", www.operamauritius.com). It seems that the repertoire included *La Bohème*, *Le Barbier de Séville*, *La Veuve joyeuse*, *Le Pays du sourire*, *Rigoletto* and *Aïda*. And that the press ensured media coverage of these events and the Mauritian socialite. By the last quarter of the 19th century, night trains were available to opera patrons to allow them to return home to the neighbouring towns after performances. As teenagers, we experienced our first taste of culture by going to a couple of these performances with some of our adult relatives, including Tonton A. We owed our love of operas and operettas to our uncles. SanKiew and Kiewkiew often intoned arias from *La Veuve joyeuse* and *Le Pays du sourire* in their shower in the middle of our courtyard at LaBoutique (our family business).

Generally, these were the attractions in the capital city that appealed to us, but they were mainly of a "touristy" or sightseeing nature. What we enjoyed more, as children on the island, were attractions that carried an element of emotional character, so to speak. We still cannot think of events like *Les Courses* and *Fancy-Fair* without getting all nostalgic about them, for they had such an impact in our youth!

THE CHAMP DE MARS RACECOURSE IN PORT-LOUIS

When we were growing up, one of the highlights of the whole year was going to the races at the Champ de Mars in Port-Louis. Each year, towards the end of the winter months, we looked forward to the Maiden Cup race, which was the biggest race of all.

The Mauritius Turf Club, which carries a long history, organized the races. This Club was founded in 1812 by Sir Robert Townsend Farquhar, and later continued under the patronage of Colonel A. Draper who was often referred to as "The father of the Mauritius Turf Club". The course at Champ de Mars was the first racecourse of the Southern Hemisphere, and the second oldest in the world. This historical course (1,298 metres in circumference) had been a French Military Training Ground until the Mauritius Turf Club was founded. Governor Farquhar, whose wife (Maria Lautour) was of French culture, wanted to cultivate harmony between the old French colonists and the new British Administrators. He felt that introducing the convivial nature of horseracing in this former French army training spot would help him achieve this goal. To this day, Champ de Mars shows evidence of the two colonial presences: The Malartic tomb, an obelisk to the French governor Malartic (who had come to Mauritius after having been on a mission to Canada), and the statue of British King Edward VII by the sculptor Prosper d'Épinay. (Mauritius Turf Club: "History", www.mauritiusturfclub.com)

Hence, by the time we discovered the Champ de Mars in the 1950's and 1960's, horseracing on the island had already had a long established history.

It was an annual tradition with all Mauritian families to attend the Maiden Cup race in September. For my cousin N., my sister and myself, preparations for going to the races had to start in good time. What dress should we wear? Did we need to have new dresses made? The decision rested with the adults. Tante Nette being the chief organizer would orchestrate the whole event, the "before", the "during" and the "after" of the Maiden.

If required, Tante Nette's seamstress would make us a simple dress. Usually, we would wear the dress we had been given for the Chinese New Year and which we had worn to visit relatives. I remember one of those dresses very particularly. It was very exciting as it was a "ready-to-wear" one (that is, bought ready-made from the shops – something unheard of on the island at the time). It had been sent to us by one of our "rich" aunties living in South Africa. The dress was made of white tulle and there were small velvet dots appliquéd on to the material. My sister's dress had blue dots and mine had red ones. We both felt like princesses wearing fairy-tale dresses! For the Maiden, we wore patent shoes reserved for special occasions. The day before, we had polished these to a perfect shine (using Brylcreem). And having to let the hem down on a dress that had become too short, or having to cut the "toe area" on our shoes that had become too small, in no way diminished the sheer delight of preparing for the day at the races. We would have been six - seven years old when we had our first experience of going to the Maiden Cup race. The tradition would continue throughout our teenage years.

After the excitement of the preparation, at long last the day would arrive. It was a major event in our monotonous "country" life. My cousin N., my sister and I, sometimes accompanied by our younger brothers, went to Tante Nette's house early in the morning. She would take us to the Champ de Mars along Labourdonnais Street, then right onto Pope Hennessy Street that led to the racecourse. Or she might decide to take a short cut along the narrow back streets at the foot of the mountain. These streets were dusty and lined with thorny cacti. The poor and dilapidated dwellings we passed were made of rusty corrugated iron sheets. They were fronted by small yards covered in weeds and edged by scraggy bushes. We saw children in rags playing in front of those hovels, but we were so excited to be going to the races in our Sunday best that we did not have time to feel guilty at the sight of such poverty!

The first things we looked for when we reached our destination were the local cakes. There were savoury ones such as *gato-piment*s, *samosas*, *dhall pourri*, *roti manillal* and *chutney*, *voo yans*/*gato-arouille*; and sweet ones such as *gato-patate* (yam cakes), and *calamindas* (candy floss also known as "father's beard"), slices of maize pudding, *gato-moutaille* saturated with syrup. We also relished in such delicacies as bags of roasted or boiled monkey nuts or peanuts. We would spend the whole day feasting on these, as well as other *gonages* (snacks including junk foods) on offer: hot and sour pickled mangoes which we would dip in a mixture of sea salt and fresh chillies; succulent slices of fresh pineapple; sticks of barley sugar; dark Chinese jelly that we savoured slowly.

At our age, the races meant only things that would excite children and youngsters. The occasional glimpse of the horses took second place. Balloons of all colours and shapes floated amongst the *Patang* or *Reine-des-airs* kites that flew above our heads. The whole sunny atmosphere of Port Louis was filled with multi-coloured confetti. We were so excited that we were almost dancing, skipping from one merry-go-round to another, surrounded by the wonderful and special aromas of all the exotic food around us. The noise of firecrackers would occasionally interrupt the joyful shouts of excited children riding horses on the colourful merry-go-rounds.

On one of those Maiden days, being in a "loge" deprived us of the delights to be found outside on the lawns. Tante Nette had taken us to visit one of her friends who was watching the races from her private "loge". These "loges" affording an unrestricted view of the course belonged to the privileged class of society. The ladies were dressed like royalty! The younger girls wore fine crocheted gloves, be-ribboned hats and shiny patent matching shoes. The women wore big elegant hats like those worn at the Ascot racecourse in England, just like those we saw in British magazines later on in life.

FANCY-FAIR IN PORT-LOUIS

We could never mention the Maiden Cup race without thinking of our other big annual event in Port Louis, the Fancy-Fair. We went to the Fair in the 1950's and 1960's. It was held on the grounds of the Loreto Convent School to raise funds, mainly for the "missions".

As Tante Nette was a teacher at the school and was one of the principal organizers, we went to help her every year. We got to the school very early in the morning to set up her stall where she sold the wares that she and her team had been making over a whole year: embroidered table cloths, colourful aprons, knitted baby garments, smocking dresses for babies and girls, and other beautiful items. She also sold home-baked cakes provided by the parishioners. We helped all day, selling the items on display and later in the afternoon, we would help Tante Nette's team draw the winning tickets for the tombola. It was great fun to see who had won which prizes. As all proceeds went to the missions, we felt good that our hard work and our few small coins were going towards a good cause.

There were food stalls selling delicious Chinese snacks such as *voo yans,* fried noodles, fried *meefoun* and other delicacies. A stall we never failed to visit was the one selling "surprises". These were small parcels in the shape of Christmas crackers, wrapped in colourful Crepe paper and tied at both ends with pretty ribbons. The pleasure was two-fold. The first one was to take as much care as possible when unwrapping the surprise, hoping to salvage as much of the paper as we could so we could re-use it, and also save the ribbons that could be used for our hair. The second thrill was to discover what surprise we had got inside the package! The usual items were: pretty handkerchiefs with a flower embroidered on them, perfumed soaps, colourful fans.

Although the focus of the day was to raise money for charities, it was also a great social occasion. For by the 1960's, we had become teen-agers and we looked forward to meeting our friends who hailed from all parts of the island. It was above all an opportunity to see the boys we admired, from the various Sino-Mauritian Clubs (the C.S.A and the Chinese Circle). We also loved to listen to the live band playing all the popular songs of the time (*Il y a le ciel, le soleil et la mer*, *Love me tender*, and so forth). We would stay until quite late but had to leave before dusk.

At the end of the day, whether it was after the Maiden Cup race or the Fancy-Fair, we had to walk to the bus terminal. We hardly had the strength to reach the bus stop to catch our bus home to Quatre-Bornes or Beau-Bassin (if we were going back to Coocoo's house, for our big cousin N. was always with us on those special occasions). Our feet were sore after the long day's activities. Our shoes did not help at all: they felt too tight more often than not. Our stomach felt a bit fragile too after eating all the *gonages* during the day. The journey back was always imbued with sadness and nostalgia. At night, when we were in bed, we would re-live those moments of great pleasure we had experienced in the capital, moments that had allowed us to leave behind, for a few hours, the somewhat monotonous life of shopkeepers' children we lived in the country-side.

Even today something as insignificant as a whiff of the delicious aroma of a *gato-piment* or *samosa*, or a simple request to buy a tombola ticket, never fails to take me back to my childhood and adolescence, to the special moments at the Maiden Cup race or at the Fancy-Fair, where it had been possible to feel almost grown-up, especially in later years, such was the sense of great freedom and adventure we experienced each year at those events.

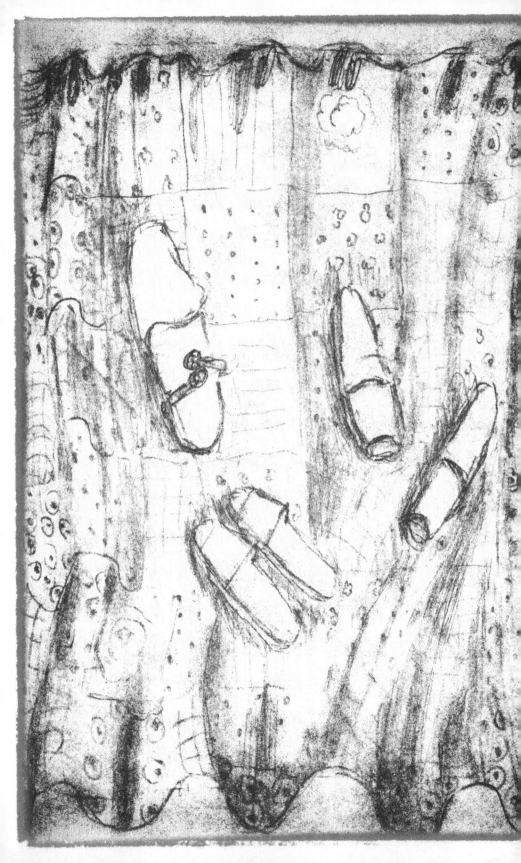

25

Ng Bhor and her Cousins

In the late 40's, when we were still living in Rose Hill, I remember that Ng Bhor (Ah Bhor, for us her grandchildren) often visited us. She was my father's mother. Her cousins frequently accompanied her.

They usually arrived at mid-day, sometimes after walking for a couple of hours. They had very early in the morning left their place of departure (Beau-Bassin, or the suburbs of Rose-Hill - Stanley, Sainte-Anne or Plaisance). They seemed old enough to us at the time, but in truth, they would have been only in their fifties.

Ah Bhor and her cousins belonged to the *Fengshun* community of Hakkas, specifically from the village of Fengliang. I remember that the ones who accompanied her more often were Ah T'ai and Ah Zee Bhor. They would visit us for several days on end. But there were other cousins like Soon Coo Bhor or Ten Sook Bhor who would come with her only for the day. The latter, we would at times visit in their shops in Curepipe or Moka. The cousins considered themselves almost like sisters, although they were only cousins, and some of them quite remotely related. At the time, all members of the community considered themselves to be close, whatever the degree of blood relationship; such was the spirit of solidarity that prevailed among all the "older generation" of Chinese immigrants on the island. Their hard lives warranted a certain degree of interdependence. Their support of each other helped them survive.

Even at our young age, we noticed a couple of distinctive traits to the Fengshun community. The physical characteristics of Ah Bhor's people seemed to us children very different from those of Maman's cultural group who came from *Moyenne* (Meixian), hardly a hundred kilometres from Fengshun. Whereas Young Bhor's family had an ivory complexion, Ng Bhor's people had a reddish complexion. When we grew older, we thought that they looked more like the Aboriginal people of North America than the "typical Chinese women". In general, it seemed to us that Ah Bhor and her cousins had a bigger bone structure than their *Moyenne* counterparts perhaps due to the work the Fengshun women did in the fields. Another distinction was in terms of language. One distinctive feature of the Fengshun dialect was the frequent "Zhi" sound, in place of the "yee" sound in Maman's dialect.

Ah Bhor's community had a mountain culture, as many other Hakkas whose villages were situated in mountainous or hilly neighbourhoods in China. Hence the traditional *San goh* (mountain song) performed from hill to hill. Whenever Ah Bhor and her cousins arrived, they brought in with them this mountain air, pure and rustic, like themselves, beautiful "women of the fields" that they were! It was a known fact that Hakka women in Fengshun and elsewhere, many of whom had to work in the fields, never had to bind their feet, unlike the women of other communities in China who were forced to such a practice from around the 11th century to the beginning of the 20th century. All Hakka women were therefore famous for being "liberated" women who were free to roam the fields and the towns as they wished.

Spontaneously cheery, the Fengshun cousins were quite loud, and would chatter away late in the night in the bed next to ours – we had all crammed into one bed to free the other for them. We as children understood most of their dialect, though we hardly spoke it. During their stay, there would be a sort of pyjama party every night, albeit amongst old women whose faces were wrinkled and weather-beaten.

Now that I think of them, it seems to me that they formed a kind of "sisterhood", of which our Ah Bhor was the natural leader, with her innate social grace, *savoir-faire*, and organizational skills. No man ever accompanied them during those visits. They were women who went out on their own, and fended for themselves during their long walks and their stays away from their homes.

What did they talk about? I cannot recall all the details but they often spoke of the past in China. Young as we were, we understood the gist of what they discussed. But years later, we came to learn how the political upheavals in China, that is, the civil wars of the 1920's to the 1940's, and the Japanese invasion of the 1930's, caused mass migrations, and forced hundreds of thousands of their compatriots to leave their ancestral home for faraway climes, including Mauritius.

During these conversations, again and again, as a perpetual reminiscence, the subject of their village in China resurfaced. How they as youngsters or grown women had helped to defend their village, hurling large rocks and heavy stones on the neighbouring invaders. One favourite topic was the hot water spring that helped them "cook" the fish for their meals. And how beautiful to us children were the mountain songs (the *San goh*)! With what nostalgia they sang these to themselves and to us children; those songs that during their years in their village, they had heard the youth sing to their beloved ones who lived on the neighbouring hills!

In their long chats, they discussed their past. How they arrived under difficult circumstances on the island, as most immigrants did at the time. They also talked about their current lives; and their living with their adult children now that they had no youngsters left at home to raise. They had settled down with one of them but rotated and stayed for some time with the others.

Ah T'ai was the cousin with a "funny" eye: she had one good eye, and one "shut" eye, which looked like a stitched scar. So, we children were a bit afraid of her; we thought she looked quite scary. She was also supposed to be able to see "spirits" around herself and others. Some years later, when we were older, she told us that she had "seen" the ghost of my other grandmother (Young Bhor) in our bedroom behind our shop in Quatre-Bornes. She generally had a lot of spooky stories that she shared with Ah Bhor and the other cousins. In spite of ourselves, we heard her eerie stories in the middle of the night: these gave us goose pumps and kept us from sleeping.

They generally stayed a few nights, and then moved on to one of their other children's houses. They seemingly moved from home to home, travelling, walking from place to place. Since they were "country" women in spirit, they did not seem to mind the miles and the constant exposure to the sun while walking in the heat of the tropics. They were indeed among the first "women trekkers" of the island at the time!

What did they wear? I remember most of them wearing the traditional black *samfoo* made with cotton fabric – set of pants and Chinese top. But Ah Bhor, after a few decades on the island, had begun to wear just a plain dark long skirt and top in the summer; she added a cardigan in the winter months. She dressed up, as years went by, in a more "Europeanized" fashion than her cousins and friends. Her daughters who had married South-African Hakkas sent these European clothes to her. In the early days, these women were usually clad in Chinese shoes; for their lengthy walks those were made sturdier than the simple light cotton house-shoes. Then later, they adopted the *"Fan gnin"* (Western people's) shoes made of light leather, and more appropriate for their long treks.

What did they do all day when they stayed? I know that their chatter lasted all day, while they performed various tasks. As to their activities, a myriad of things come to mind. Did they sew us clothes? Indeed, in the winter, we all benefitted from these special Chinese padded jackets that were so warm, and we all made good use of the crocheted woollen blankets. And these women knew how to make Chinese *K'iaks* (wooden clogs), which they carved with little chisels to make them for the adults of the family for their bath-time. They also made preserves with mustard greens to make *Ham Choy* or *Kon Ham Choy*. We loved watching them macerate these greens on a board with handfuls of sea-salt, to pickle them or hang them to dry on ropes in the tropical sun. In addition, they cooked us those delicious Fengshun dishes (like the crystal noodles made sugary with a nice syrupy sauce, or made spicy with very hot mustard).

I can recall that Ah Bhor oftentimes led the group in some of those activities, and other types of hobbies. One of these was the making of quilts (a simplified version). I seem to recall her and her cousins sitting with a central basket filled with all sorts of rags and remnants of material, and cutting squares or triangles from them. These cuttings were then harmoniously sewn together (either manually or with a machine) to make a bed cover for one of their children. The product, which would last us whole decades, would always be a delight to look at, with a kaleidoscopic result: a constellation of colours, patterns, and textures.

The closeness of these women to each other, and the harmonious way they functioned together, as well as the manner in which they handled their lives, more often than not without a man to support them, certainly constituted an early form of "feminism". Even in cases when they still had a husband, they seemed to have been the moral force of the family unit, armed with the strength and endurance that their upbringing and, over the years, their hard lives had yielded.

Indeed, these women symbolized an early type of modernity. They were already the modern independent women, at a time when feminism in Mauritius was at its very early inception. Later on, we noted that they had been an interesting combination of "old" and "new". Their attitude and vision were relatively "new" on our small island, but this was mixed with the "ancient": they still had the traditional Confucian family and community values, and the old look with their dark-coloured attire, their distinguished greying hair neatly tucked in at the nape by a large antique Chinese barrette.

Ah Bhor and her cousins will always be to us, the grand-children, the epitome of the clan mentality: that of a community of migrants who have survived on account of the fortitude and solidarity prevailing amongst its members, and more particularly, amid its women. Indeed, the community spirit has survived through many generations thanks to these remarkable women of the past: their lives, their very deeds. Their children and their descendants will not readily forget them.

26

CYCLONE CAROL

The heat is suffocating during the summer of 1960. The adults are all thinking: yes, it would not be surprising if a cyclone were on its way. True enough, after a few days of torrid heat, there are cyclone warnings on the radio. Bad luck indeed, as our little island has been hit by Cyclone Alix barely a month before. Alix has left in its wake 30,000 refugees, after the destruction of more than 25,000 buildings. Our sugar cane industry has been affected: we expect a drop of 50% in revenue.

And here is Cyclone Carol coming from the island of Saint Brandon. Following a southerly course, it hits Mauritius on February 26th and is with us until February 28th; the "eye" of the cyclone takes four long hours to move across the island. After the lull during the eye's trajectory, the gusts of wind and lashing rain come back stronger than ever.

Gale force winds of 256 kms per hour rage over the island for several days. Our sugar cane plantations suffer 60% loss and our tea plantations 30%. The devastation is complete. It is chaos!! The British Media and others describe this cyclone as the most disastrous to have struck the Indian Ocean in modern history. ("Les Cyclones les plus dévastateurs", L'Express, 13 janvier 2015)

The report issued by the British House of Lords in March 1960, states that this cyclone has caused 42 deaths, and 1,700 injuries (95 of which are severe); 100,000 houses and buildings have been destroyed and, out of a population of 600,000, more than 70,000 have sought refuge in government shelters. After the devastation caused by Cyclone Alix, it is a disastrous blow to our already vulnerable island. ("Cyclone Damages in Mauritius", Hansard, 17 March 1960)

In Quatre-Bornes, one of the most affected towns, we are shocked by the violence of the gusts of wind and the force of the torrential rain.

For our safety, we children must remain within the confines of the small house behind the shop. Outside, sheets of corrugated iron, ripped off the roofs and flying everywhere, constitute a serious danger, especially for children who are more at risk in such situations. There are reports of some people being beheaded by flying corrugated iron sheets. It seems that they went outside during the lull thinking that the cyclone had gone. They were caught out by the violent gales which generally start again, with a vengeance, as the cyclone changes direction after the lull.

Later, we hear that one of our uncles nearly got crushed by the collapsing front window of the shop. This almost fell on him while he was rescuing the goods on display in the window. Just before it happened, he saw a flash of lightning; and his mother appeared to him to warn him about the danger. He moved promptly, and miraculously, a big pillar near him stopped the window case from falling directly on him. He thus narrowly escaped a certain death!

All through these long hours, amid the howling winds that swirl like demented demons furiously attacking humans and buildings alike, adults in every family fight to save their household. As long as the roof holds above their heads, there is a chance of survival. As many other buildings on the island, our shop is old, made of wood and has a corrugated iron roof. The men tie thick ropes to their waists onto the beams supporting the ceiling in an endeavour to save the top that has started to lift off. Some of the smaller corrugated iron sheets have already been blown away. The larger ones are saved by the ropes tied to the men. These are themselves at risk of being lifted off the ground. Hence they form a chain by holding hands, to augment their weight and withstand the violence of the wind. Other ropes are secured to the ground with sacks of rice, barrels of salted fish, or other large containers full of heavy products.

Our dining room is an open space that also suffers from the fury of the gales. However, this lean-to is less vulnerable than the shop because it lies lower than the main building and is protected by it. But it is already flooded, the narrow water-duct running its whole length being inadequate for the amount of rain of the past few days. The floor of this exposed area is already littered with tins, branches and other debris blown in from the neighbourhood. We have to take care to avoid cutting ourselves on the sharp edges of the cans. Here too, thick ropes are holding the roof down but this time the ends of the ropes are secured to the legs of the heavy tables. We are able to save the main part of our shop's roof as well as that of our dining room by taking these simple but effective measures. Unfortunately our small bedroom at the back is already flooded, a huge amount of rain having come through the old and damaged roof. There is at least one foot of water inside the room. At night time, to reach the bed, we use wooden crates that Maman has placed between the door and the bed as stepping-stones.

The hours seem endless. We hear the wind and the rain crashing on the roof. It seems that we can hear, from far away, the roar of water cascading down the slopes of Colline Candos and Montagne Corps de Garde. All we can do is listen to an angry nature that unleashes enormous sheets of water, and gales that gather strength from hour to hour. Anguish reigns in the small house and in the shop. While the adults try to save the shop, we tell each other stories, or play Snake and Ladders, Carom, and other games. We do all this in semi darkness or by candlelight, as there is no electricity throughout the island. Since torn electrical live wires are a real danger inside the house and outside, the government has cut off the source of electricity for the whole population. Before we go to sleep, an adult escorts us to the outside lavatory that is in the back yard. A lantern is used to light the way. The flame is shaky and is in danger of blowing out at any moment. We walk close to each other, as near the external wall of the kitchen as we can. We cling to each other so that we are not blown away by the gale force winds. When we arrive back to the veranda there is an oil lamp welcoming us.

The bread we have is stale, and there will be no fresh bread for a several days following the cyclone. All the bakeries have been demolished by the gales, and are without electricity. Or their wood-fuelled ovens have been destroyed. When the stale bread runs out, we eat " biscuit cabine", a sort of thick cracker used in the navy that keeps fresh in the cabins (hence the name) for far longer than other biscuits. These biscuits have little holes in them, and it is said that after the first few months at sea, when the biscuits have become stale, sailors tap them before eating them to allow 'creepy crawlies" escape through the holes! Besides the stale bread and "cabine" biscuits, we have simple hot meals prepared by

Cook on a wood-burning stove: meals of rice and dried vegetables still available in the house.

After the cyclone, we are without electricity for what seems like an endless period. The battery-run radio is a most useful item. It keeps us informed of the weather forecast and other news. We listen to it regularly as we are curious to know how the other towns and villages are coping. Electric bulbs are replaced by candles or paraffin lamps. Alternative ways of cooking are found. Amongst other means, we use a Primus stove. What an invention this is! Developed by Wilhelm Lindqvist (a Swede) as early as 1892, this first pressurized-burner paraffin stove became popular during the early decades of the 20th century because it was easy to use even under the most difficult conditions. The explorers Nansen and Amundsen used it during their expeditions to the North Pole and South Pole respectively; Mallory used it during his attempt to conquer Mount Everest. It was a revolutionary invention, unlike other stoves that require a wick and produce soot. (Primus: "Our Story", http://www.primus.eu/)

Cooking is fast and easy on this light and small stove weighing only two and a half lbs., and measuring hardly eight and half inches in height and seven inches in diameter. As children, we like watching Cook fill the stove with a small amount of alcohol in the spirit cup. He then lights the alcohol to preheat the burner unit. Once the alcohol is hot, he presses the hand pump which forces the paraffin from the tank up to the burner head where the paraffin is heated and vapourized. The paraffin vapour is then forced under pressure to form gas sprays through a jet in the middle of the burner where it mixes with air and burns in a sootless blue flame; pumping the tank more increases the pressure and makes the flame larger; and turning a small air screw releases the pressure, and the flame becomes smaller. We are fascinated by the whole procedure, but we are not allowed to handle the Primus, considered too dangerous for children. And we find it a bit frightening! The use of the stove is clean and efficient and it is not surprising that, in the post-Carol months, all those who can afford it use it.

Besides the Primus, people use wood-burning stoves. They also find wood dust very useful as fuel: hence the creation of the wood-dust stoves. The wood dust is pressed into the shape of a stove with a tunnel in the centre for air to circulate. Despite our youth, we are allowed to help in the compressing process. We have a field day thumping our feet or fists onto the dust. When finished, the wood dust stove is indeed a work of art, a sculpture, no more, no less, according to us, children! We take pride in being part of the whole team: fanning the fire is great fun for some of us big enough to partake in this whole process of "allime ressaud la poussière di bois" (lighting up the wood-dust stove).

Electricity is off for several endless weeks. Ironmonger's shops selling all manner of stoves make a fortune; so do shops that sell candles and lamps. Also profiting from the situation are the importers of "Delcos" used by big businesses that need to produce their own electricity to survive.

We at LaBoutique (our family business) cannot afford a Delco. The meat products in our shop's freezers are at risk of spoiling. What can we do to salvage the situation? Our parents worry, as there is no sign that electricity will be restored. A solution has to be found. The adults quickly come up with an inspired idea, for the chicken at least: cook the chicken and sell it. Action promptly follows thought. Every adult in the shop helps to cut the chickens in portions. Maman marinates the pieces in a Chinese sauce and deep-fries them in a big wok over a wood burning stove. During the days following the cyclone, word spreads that very tasty fried chicken is being sold in our shop and at a very reasonable price. The situation is saved!

In the months following Cyclone Carol, many essential commodities like rice and flour are rationed. Vegetables and fruit are in short supply, therefore very expensive. All the vegetable gardens and orchards have been destroyed. Since almost all the fishermen's boats have been wrecked, fish supply has been affected and it is sold at a highly inflated price. Consequently, for their consumption of produce such as tomatoes, garden peas, peaches and pears, the population has to turn to frozen food and tinned food imported from South Africa, Australia, and even from as far as Great Britain and France.

After the cyclone, our young adolescent life continues despite all the deprivations. We feel happy and free as schools have closed down and are likely to be so for the foreseeable future. The two cyclones have severely damaged or completely demolished most schools. Our enforced holiday becomes exciting with the visit of our cousin M. from South Africa. He stays for a few weeks. He captivates us with his modern style, his height, his striking green eyes, and his smile. He dresses like Elvis, with tight jeans and shirt opened down to the third button. He has a crew cut like the one Elvis had when he was in the army. Our youngest aunt A. and M. have a romance. We catch them kissing behind Maman's wardrobe!

To my sister and me who are Form 2 and Form 3 pupils at the Loreto Convent, schools seem to have been closed for the longest time. We continue to attend teenage parties. We sleep over at Coocoo's when we do not want Papa to know that we are going to these parties. There, we dance twists, foxtrots and waltzes. We also go to the annual ball organized by the Chinese Circle or the CSA where we forget all about the ravage caused by the cyclones; we have fun and listen to the popular songs we love so much: *Love me Tender, Sealed with a Kiss, Are You Lonesome Tonight* ...

Everything might be destroyed around us but nothing stops us from wearing the fashionable "bouffant" knee length dresses worn over organza or tulle petticoats. We wear Ballerina shoes, Alice bands on our short and backcombed hair like Sylvie Vartan and Sandra Dee. We are more than ever influenced by European fashion through imported magazines, and later on, through television that reaches the island and changes our life. There are many foreigners on the island during the post-Carol era, and they have an impact on us too.

Indeed, our tiny nation gets all sorts of international aid. As we are still a British colony, Great Britain sends practical and financial help. The British Government sends its naval forces, including the Crown Colony-Class light cruiser (the HMS Gambia) to help us rebuild our island. The House of Lords discusses the situation, as reported in the Hansard, and agrees to finance the repairs to government buildings and the infrastructure of our country. The British Government assesses the destruction of Cyclone Carol and increases the aide of £ 2 million that they have already pledged after Cyclone Alix. France sends a school cruiser, the *Jeanne d'Arc*. Other voluntary agencies like The Red Cross come to help restore sanitary conditions and educate the population in ways of stopping Malaria and other diseases that are a real threat. Centres for refugees are built by teams of local builders (Les Compagnons

Bâtisseurs), with the help of voluntary workers from the SCI of Great Britain. Further assistance is provided by two groups from The International Organization of Voluntary Helpers. (Cyclone Carol: Sheard, Sally, *The Passionate Economist*, 2014: 167-68)

The economy of Mauritius is at rock bottom. It is a socio-economic disaster that will last many years; we depend entirely on the sugar industry and this has been ravaged by the two cyclones: sugar production constitutes 98% of our exports in the 1960's, and we stand to lose more than 50% of our sugar production.

Hence, as of 1960, many changes will occur on our island on account of Cyclone Carol. In terms of lighting and fuel, soon the use of candles, paraffin lamps, Primus and wood stoves become the norm. A bit later, those who have the means purchase gas cylinders to cook with. "Delcos" are widely available to bigger businesses to produce their own electricity. For news dissemination, we rely more and more on radios that can run on batteries. On the whole, we shy away from anything that runs on electricity.

Those are the short term consequences of the historic cyclone. In the long term, Cyclone Carol is indirectly responsible for precipitating Mauritius into modernity.

There will be a gradual modernization of the building industry. The urban and rural landscape changes completely after this historic event: since concrete can withstand the ravages of gale force winds and torrential rain, little by little, cement buildings replace wooden structures and their corrugated iron roofs. As entire villages have been flattened, residents slowly replace their huts with concrete houses, sometimes adding only a cement room at a time, gradually replacing the damaged wooden hut.

During the months and years following the cyclone, the landscape will change from total chaos to a semblance of recovery and relative stability. Les Compagnons Bâtisseurs led by Edwin de Robillard will build shelters for more than 70,000 refugees. These shelters called "Longères" or "Cases-poteaux" (small rudimentary constructions) are built with the financial assistance of The Sugar Industries Labour Welfare Fund, the Gulbenkian Foundation, and other agencies. The "Longères" will be part of the Mauritian landscape for a long time. Over the years, these will gradually be replaced by concrete buildings. Hence the emergence of housing estates like Cité Candos and Cité Kennedy in parts of the island.

The years following Cyclone Carol will bring many social changes too. A whole generation is born to marriages or liaisons between Mauritian women and men from the foreign voluntary workers agencies, the British forces, the American businesses, and other international agencies.

The modernization of the island continues. Lifestyle is changing: beside transistor radios, L.P. music records and Formica become an integral part of our everyday life. As regards telecommunication, new weather satellites are introduced in April 1960. It is a radical improvement, since during Cyclone Carol, observations of the weather were carried out from ships or faraway islands. Television comes to the nation soon after, to become a permanent fixture to our society. In our own family, we benefitted from a prototype set ingeniously assembled by our uncle Sessouk, which he brought back from England after his Engineering studies there.

We question our entire dependency on the sugar industry in the aftermath of Cyclone Carol. We realize that our monoculture economy bears too much risk: a system of diversification is planned and slowly put into action.

The post-Carol years see the gradual emergence of a variety of industries throughout the island thanks to local and foreign investments. The next decade witnesses the start of a gigantic growth in the textile industry and the creation of the "Zone Franche" (Free Zone), resulting between 1970 and 1980 in the creation more than 20,000 new jobs. This was made possible by the increase in numbers, from 138 to 563, of foreign and local businesses in our newly industrialized island. (Cyclone Carol: Grégoire, Emmanuel, "La Migration des emplois à l'Ile Maurice", 2006: 56-57)

The development of the island progresses rather quickly. A better road system is needed to transport the new products. The motorway linking Phoenix to Port Louis is built, a symbol of the propulsion of our small island into modernity. Economy booms over the following decades.

In 1975, intense Cyclone Gervaise hits the island with gale force winds of 280 kms per hour. Less devastation is experienced than in 1960 because a great percentage of houses has already been rebuilt in concrete. As well, with a diversified economy, we feel less severely the damage to the sugar industry.

It is evident that Cyclone Carol has been a pivotal event in the socio-economic history of the island. It remains a vital part of the collective consciousness of Mauritians who have lived through this memorable cyclone and its aftermath. Sharing difficulties in a stressful situation unites a nation. The atmosphere of risks, grave danger and hardship has made us stand together in solidarity on this island so tiny, so remote in the middle of the ocean, and so vulnerable in the face of the devastating effects of the elements. It can be said that this disaster has made us more patriotic. Through this very traumatic experience, we have moved up a step on our existential journey as a nation, and reached the age of reason. For indeed, after Cyclone Carol, have we not as Mauritians "come of age"!

FURTHER READING

Beau-Bassin-Rose Hill: "History",
http://bbrh.org/
(Retrieved: 2016)
http://unhabitat.org/
(Retrieved: 2012)

Bhikkhuni Dhammananda, The history of the bhikkhuni sangha in *Blossoms of the Dharma—Living as a Buddhist Nun*, (Dec 28, 1999), www.thubtenchodron.org/1992/12/enlightenment-women/
(Retrieved: 2016)

Ceremonies and Funeral Rites for the Dead,
http://www.buddhanet.net/d_cermon.htm
(Retrieved: 2012)

Ces Crimes les plus marquants: "Le Crime de la Citadelle"
(3 janvier 2017),
www.lexpress.mu,
(Retrieved: 2017)

Chinese New Year History,
www.chinesenewyears.info/Chinese-new-year-history.php
(Retrieved: 2017)

Cyclone Carol:
"Cyclone Damages in Mauritius",
(HANSARD 1803–2005, 1960s, 1960, March 1960, 17 March 1960),
http://hansard.millbanksystems.com/sittings/1960/mar/17
(Retrieved: 2016)

"Les Cyclones les plus dévastateurs", *L'Express* (13 janvier 2015), www.lexpress.mu
(Retrieved: 2016)
Sheard, Sally, *The Passionate Economist*, 2014 : 167-68.

Fillion, Jean-Michel, "La Traite vers l'Ile de France" in *Slavery in the South-West Indian Ocean*
Mauritius: Mahatma Gandhi Institute, 1989.

Grégoire, Emmanuel, "La Migration des emplois à l'Ile Maurice: La filière textile et les entreprises", in *Savoir et Développement*, 2006.

"Hakka Women: Transforming Images of the Hakka", *Christian Souls and Chinese Spirits*,
http://publishing.cdlib.org/
(Retrieved: 2016)

Jessop, Arthur, *A History of the Mauritius Government Railways, 1864-1964*, Port Louis: J. Eliel Felix, Government Printer (OCLC 636712).

Kalla, A. Cader, "Reverend Lebrun as Pedagogue", July 2, 2014, www.lemauricien.com,

Li Tio Fane Pineo, Huguette, *La Diaspora chinoise dans l'Océan Occidental*, Aix-en-Provence: Institut d'Histoire des Pays d'Outremer (Gréco-Océan Indien), Mauritius: Mahatma Gandhi Institute, 1981.

Li Tio Fane Pineo, Huguette, *Lured Away: The Life History of Indian Cane Workers in Mauritius*, Mauritius: Mahatma Gandhi Institute, 1984.

Loreto Convents,
www.ibvm.org
www.loreto.ie
Institute of the Blessed Virgin Mary (Loreto Sisters):
"The First Loreto Community in Mauritius, 2014",
www.ibvm.org/?s=history+of+IBVM+schools
"History of Loreto in Curepipe »,

http://vintagemauritius.org/
(Websites retrieved: 2016)

Mauritius Turf Club : "History",
www.mauritiusturfclub.com
(Retrieved: 2016)

Municipal Council of Quatre-Bornes: "History of Quatre-Bornes",
http://www.qb.mu/
(Retrieved 2012)

Noël, Karl, *L'Esclavage à l'Isle de France (Ile Maurice) de 1715 à 1810*,
Paris: Ed. Two Cities ETC, 1991.

Port Louis, Mauritius (ca. 1650-),
http://www.blackpast.org/gah/port-louis-mauritius-1968
(Retrieved: 2017)

Port Louis, The Municipal Theatre,
www.vintagemauritius.org
www.operamauritius.com
(Websites retrieved: 2017)

Primus: "Our Story",
http://www.primus.eu/
(Retrieved: 2016)

"Sino-Japanese Wars",
https://www.britannica.com/event/Sino-Japanese-War-1937-1945
(Retrieved: 2016)

Trans-Atlantic Slave Trade,
The Slave Route: Trade in the Indian Ocean,
www.unesco.org
(Retrieved: 2017)

BACK COVER

17884796R00115

Printed in Poland
by Amazon Fulfillment
Poland Sp. z o.o., Wrocław